A BRIDE'S EDITION

WESTERN DESTINIES

BLYTHE CARVER

1

Luke Turner could hardly believe his eyes. At this time last year, he and his best friend, Dylan Sullivan, had been looking into ways to get the money together to start a magazine. Now they were sitting in the office of Judge Carter Holbrook while he outlined papers approving financial backing for their magazine, though it was no longer a magazine based on men and politics.

It had taken some convincing, but Luke and Mattie, Dylan's new wife, who just happened to be the daughter of the Honorable Judge Holbrook, had gotten Dylan on board with a magazine for mail order brides, which was all the rage, especially in Bighorn Texas other Western states. There weren't enough women, it was clear to see, and men were desperate to have wives and families.

At the same time, immigrants were coming across the eastern border, and South Carolina, Virginia, and New York were gradually becoming overpopulated. Women wanted a way out. It seemed like a win-win situation to Luke and Mattie.

"Here you go," Judge Holbrook said, sliding the papers in their direction across the surface of his desk. "All signed and ready to go. You take this to the bank, and they'll open an account for your expenses. You'll have this much here," he tapped his pen on the paper over a number he'd written, "to use for starting up and getting that second printing press you require. You will need to get two more employees to run the press without a lot of stress. You'll also want to get some females to write advertisements. Men don't know what to say, do they?" He cracked a grin.

Luke and Dylan returned his smile. Luke let his friend get the documents first. This was Dylan's dream, his baby. Even though Luke would be doing most of the work, he knew how much having the new magazine up and running meant to Dylan.

"I don't know how to thank you enough, Judge Holbrook," Dylan said, lifting up from the chair and leaning over the desk, one hand extended. The judge also stood up and took his son-in-law's hand.

"Just don't ever call me Pops, and we will get along just fine." The judge laughed, slapping his other hand on Dylan's elbow as he shook his hand.

The two men laughed in a way that made Luke feel a little left out. Not because he was insecure but just because he realized the two of them were actually relatives, and he was the third wheel.

Luke was not in any way an insecure man. He just wasn't used to not having Dylan as his sidekick. Since he married, Luke had, of course, seen him much less than he had before. He and Dylan had been living together. Dylan had recently purchased a ranch—which was why Luke would be doing most of the work at the magazine—and he lived there with Mattie. Luke expected soon they would start a family, and he would never see Dylan again.

Unless he also had a family.

Luke had no prospects for marriage, though he was a popular and friendly man.

Dylan pulled him out of his thoughts by turning and resting a firm hand on his shoulder. "We're going to make this magazine a success, aren't we?"

Luke nodded, deciding now was the perfect time for his surprise. He reached under the chair he was sitting in and pulled out a cloth sack he'd brought in when they entered. He set it carefully on the desk between them with a beaming smile.

"I've brought something to celebrate our new partnership, Judge Holbrook. I hope you don't mind."

"Don't mind a bit," the judge said, delight in his voice and a sparkle in his eye when he saw Luke pull a bottle of imported champagne from the cloth bag. It was in its own bag to keep it from breaking. "I assume you have some glasses we can use? I'm afraid I wasn't bold enough to bring them along with me for fear they would shatter."

Dylan winked at him, his own grin wide and amused. Luke popped open the champagne while the judge turned to his mini-bar and grabbed three glasses from the cabinet hanging above it.

Luke poured until their glasses were three-quarters full and set the bottle down with vehement exuberance. He held his glass up in the air. "To Bridal Bliss," he announced loudly, "and to new partnerships."

His two companions repeated the words, and they all drank to the new magazine. Luke was looking forward to the work. He'd been lacking much to do recently, especially with Dylan spending his time with his wife at his new ranch.

Luke didn't know it was possible to be as bored as he was without Dylan to have adventures with. He wouldn't have minded having a woman on his arm, but that seemed like a pipe dream to him. He was a confident man. He knew there was nothing wrong with him physically. He was smart and strong.

And now he was the part-owner of a mail order bride magazine. What could be better than that? It was like God just dropped the opportunity in his lap, like an answer to his prayers.

He would place his own ad. Test out their system.

Maybe he would find love.

2

The sound of his boots on the wooden floor echoed through the room when Luke stepped inside. There was a commotion in the back, where men were placing the two printing presses next to each other. More men maneuvered around the others, placing tables, chairs, and equipment all around where the working staff would be.

He was in the front room, the main office where people would come in and be greeted by their receptionist, a woman he had yet to hire. That was something he wanted to talk to Dylan about.

The main room was the last one that would be furnished. Luke went across the empty room to one of the doors, the one with his name painted in fancy letters on the foggy blown glass that made up the upper half. He admired his name for a moment before opening the door and going in.

Together, the partners had decided to get rid of all their old furniture and buy everything new. The judge had provided enough capital for them to expand a lot. Luke was filled with excitement just from gazing at his new office.

He strolled across the lengthy room and sat in the big desk chair he'd chosen. It swiveled in a circle, so he was able to look out the window behind him with ease. They had a new corner building now, and he could see all four sides of the intersection from that window. It would come in handy for days when he just wanted to observe what was going on in his little part of town.

"Like what you see?" He spun back around when he heard Dylan's voice. His partner stood at the door, leaning on the jamb, his thumbs stuck in his suspenders.

"I do like it, Dylan. I like it a lot. How about you? You like your office?"

"Yeah," he responded with little enthusiasm, shrugging his shoulders as he entered the room. He dropped into the chair across the desk from Luke and grinned. "I just don't think I'll be in there much. I've got an office at the ranch, too, and still have a lot of stuff over there at the house, you know, where you..." He waved his hand in Luke's general direction.

He and Dylan had been sharing a house before Dylan met Mattie and married her. Office things weren't the only items he'd left behind when he moved to the ranch. Most of Dylan's life was in the house Luke still occupied, which was fine with Luke. His friend was welcome to leave behind whatever he wanted. It would be kept safe until he came to retrieve whatever it might be.

"Yes, yes," Luke replied, nodding. "At least you know it's there if you need it."

Dylan chuckled. "I'll just tell you now, though, that if something important comes for me in the post or someone comes looking for me, you'll want to notify me at the ranch. That's probably where I'll be. There really is so much that needs to be done there. You'd be surprised."

Luke nodded, but he was pretty sure he wouldn't be surprised. He hadn't been raised on a ranch, but he'd worked several summers on various ranches around Texas and knew it was not a small task to run one of them. Dylan was lucky enough to have inherited a foreman who had been there for a long time and knew what he was doing.

What remained unspoken between them was Dylan's need for the magazine to be a success. He'd invested all his money in the ranch, and his wife had to match what he put in, so technically, she owned half the ranch, too. Mattie was a hardworking, fiery type of woman, so Luke was sure she would put her all into making the ranch a success.

Thinking about Mattie reminded Luke of his plan. He had yet to tell Dylan about it and thought it was the perfect time to do so.

"I'm gonna put my own ad in our magazine," he said bluntly, his eyes directly on his friend to see his reaction.

Dylan's eyes lit up with interest, and his eyebrows lifted. He sat forward. "Is that so?" he asked, one side of his lips pulling back.

Luke nodded. "Yeah. In the first edition we send out. It's gonna be a skeleton magazine to start with, you know. Mostly articles about the mail order bride business, and I'm trying to get some success stories, but they aren't exactly pouring in, you know. You want to look at the concept?"

Dylan nodded, reaching under his chair and pulling it forward more so he was right at the desk.

Luke opened the drawer at his chest and withdrew a folder. He lifted the top and began to spread out the papers so Dylan could see it, page by page.

His eyes on the papers, he tapped one by one as he spoke. "This is the front. You can see this is just a blank picture for now. That's just a design I scribbled to take up the space for the front picture. This is how the title will be. Do you like that? We can change it to look two other ways."

Dylan nodded. "I like that."

Luke went through the rest of the pages, showing Dylan what the end result would be.

"As you can tell, this is for when we start actually having something to fill the magazine with." Luke removed several of the pages and set them aside. He pulled the remaining ones closer together. "This is what the first one will look like. Or thereabouts. This is the last page here. On the inside will be advertise-ments for the two new job positions. I thought if a woman didn't have an incentive to marry, perhaps she would need a job."

Dylan gave him a big smile. "That's brilliant, Luke. I knew there was a reason I wanted to go into business with you. You've always been smarter than me."

Luke snorted. "I don't know if I'd say that." He

began to gather the papers together to tuck away back in the folder.

"Sure you would," Dylan laughed as he spoke. "I'm saying you look at your brain and what you come up with, and I'll execute it, right? I'll make sure the brawn comes into this, right?"

He laughed, and Luke couldn't help laughing with him. Dylan lifted one arm and made a muscle, which couldn't be seen beneath the fabric of his white shirt. He waved dismissively and laughed in a lighthearted tone.

"You want any advice on what to write in your advertisement, you just ask Mattie. She knows how to appeal to a woman, you know. Take my advice. She tells me all the time how I can get better."

Luke reacted with surprise. He had never gotten the impression that Mattie was much of a dictator or a teacher. Dylan saw the look and laughed.

"Trust me, it's for my own good. She's not a nag, thank the Lord." He crossed himself while looking upwards, "but she does like to point things out that I need to know. I gotta say she was never wrong."

"I may have to get Mattie to coach the woman I bring over from the East."

Dylan snorted this time, and Luke was caught off

guard. The sound was so funny, he let out an abrupt laugh.

"What did I say?" he asked.

"You're not askin' for much, are you?" Dylan responded, giving his friend a direct look. "Try bringing a woman over and then telling her to be more like a woman that's already here. I'd love it if Mattie could be friends with the lady. That won't happen if you go and do something like that."

Luke laughed. "I see your point. I'll try to make sure they are suitable to me before they get out over here."

Dylan nodded at him, but Luke could see the regretful look on his friend's face.

"Don't worry about me," he said, trying to ease his friend's mind. "I won't be lonely and alone forever. I'll find my woman. I just have to be patient."

3

———

uke skipped the first two steps of the porch steps as he went up. His long legs had him across the porch in a few seconds. He could hear men shouting out near the backyard, so he headed through the house to the large office Dylan had given himself.

He was impressed with the office once again, just like he had been the first time he went in. There were three windows, as well as double glass doors that let out onto a long, wide veranda. Dylan had placed outside furniture all around the veranda for the parties he and his wife planned to have.

Dylan was sitting at one of those tables right at that moment, holding a glass with a amber-colored liquid in it as he watched the action below him. He turned swiftly when he heard Luke come through the doorway and shot to his feet.

"Luke. Good to see you. Do you have it?"

The way he whirled around and approached Luke with an excited look made Luke smile. He held out the thin magazine. It was only six pages with a front and back cover. But it was their first production, and he was proud of what it looked like.

Dylan snatched it from him and held it at arm's length between both hands. He gazed at the front cover with pride. "Would you look at that," he exclaimed. He smiled wide at Luke, slapping the front cover with the fingers of one hand. "We did that, didn't we? We did it."

Luke chuckled. "Yep. That's our product right there."

"Now, may we make lots and lots of money from it," Dylan continued, looking up as if praying the words directly to God.

Luke walked with Dylan back to the table he'd been seated at while his friend fingered through the pages. "It's not big, but it looks quality," Dylan murmured appreciatively. "Who did you get to do the cover art after all?"

Luke had asked some of the local amateur artists to draw something for the cover of the first magazine. He'd made it into a competition, and the winner won a dollar as well as having their artwork displayed on the magazine cover.

"June Appleseed," he replied. "She does some great work, doesn't she?"

Dylan nodded. "She sure does," he murmured. Luke could tell by the way he was eyeing the magazine he was looking for errors or mistakes. That was the only time he looked that intensely at anything.

They both sat down, and Luke looked out over the green backyard, admiring the beauty of the landscape. "What are they doing down there?" It was really a rhetorical question. He could see they were building a gazebo. It looked to be one of the larger ones, too. He assumed Mattie meant for it to be another place for parties. She did enjoy entertaining other people.

"Building a new gazebo to Mattie's exact specifications," Dylan replied under his breath, his eyes still on the magazine. He flipped to the last page and ran his eyes over the advertisements. "Hard to believe there's not a soul in town interested in working at our magazine."

"I don't think it has anything to do with us," Luke replied. "I'd rather have fresh faces in the job anyway. Everybody in Bighorn knows about the magazine.

Some of those ladies don't want anything to do with it. They say it's a sinful way to get a spouse."

Dylan wrinkled his nose. "Ah, what do they know? They're probably old biddies that have been married for a hundred years. They don't know how hard it is to find a woman in this day and age."

"Especially out here."

"You know, they say Texas has more women in it than any other western state."

Luke gave his friend an interested look. "That so? Then where are they? They should be knockin' down my door right now. I don't believe it."

Dylan sat back, slapping the magazine down on the table and laughing. "Well, good, because I just made that up. Right in here." He tapped the side of his head. Luke gave him a narrow look and shook his head.

"Oh yeah, I meant to ask if you put your ad in here." Dylan scooped the magazine back up and flipped through it, running his eyes down the two columns of advertisements Luke had been able to garner before the magazine was printed. "Ah, there it is. Handsome, wealthy bachelor looking for a beautiful, quiet woman to do whatever she's told—"

Luke snatched the magazine from his friend.

"That's not what it says," he bellowed and swatted at Dylan, who ducked away, laughing. Luke had to make sure it didn't say that as a joke and was relieved to see his ad was exactly how he'd written it. "Don't scare me like that, Dylan. I don't know what you get up to when you start feeling crazy."

Dylan just laughed some more, shaking his head. "I wouldn't do that to you, Luke. You're a good man, and you deserve a good woman. Now that I've got Mattie, I know you gotta be lonely."

Luke didn't look at Dylan but could feel his friend's eyes on him. "Don't get me wrong. I'm not sayin' you don't have any other friends or have interesting things to do. I just know how I would feel if the shoes were on my feet and you'd found a woman, got married, and moved out."

Luke glanced at Dylan. "Yeah, I see how happy you are, and I'll admit I'd like to have that for myself. That's why I put the ad in, I guess. But I'm not jealous of ya. I wouldn't take all this away from you and keep it for myself. I'm happy for you, Dylan. I really am."

Dylan nodded. He'd returned his gaze to the men working on the gazebo, listening to them yell instructions to each other as the walls went up. "I know, buddy. And I'm hopin' you find the woman of your dreams. You never know. It could happen."

"I'm just glad there's a chance to meet someone new," Luke responded, settling into the chair. "I'm looking forward to it."

"That's the spirit." Dylan lifted his glass from the tabletop and realized Luke had nothing to drink. "Well, I'm a terrible host, ain't I? You want somethin' to drink?"

Luke grinned. "You're not used to treating me like a guest," he suggested. "I'll get something. You stay right here."

"You're never a guest in my house," Dylan called out as Luke went back inside. Before he crossed through, he heard Dylan say to himself, "Wait, that didn't sound right. He is a guest, but he's family, so he's not a guest..."

His voice trailed off as Luke got out of earshot. It really was a very nice ranch house. It was bigger than the one they had shared, of course, but not by a whole lot. Luke's house was left to him by a relative he hadn't even known. Since he and Dylan had been friends for as long as Luke could remember, he had invited his friend to stay while they worked on their growing business together.

Now the two were fully invested in their new

lives—Dylan with the ranch and his wife, Luke with the magazine. He would keep himself busy doing interviews, proofreading, and probably maintaining the presses, as well.

By the time he got back outside with a drink, Dylan had left the veranda. He'd taken the large stone steps down to the ground and walked over to the construction work on the veranda. He was talking to several of the workers, who were smiling at him and nodding.

4

———

Isabella—Izzie—Russo stepped off the boat, doing her best to compose herself as she walked down the plank to the busy platform. The dock was filled with men of all shapes and sizes. She could hear their loud voices calling out to each other, laughter rang through the air, the sound of anger following it close behind.

Izzie's heart slammed in her chest. She was just glad she didn't have to struggle to understand the words she heard all around her.

Izzie and her younger brother, Lorenzo affection-ately called Lo, had just come from a small village in Italy, where they had been raised by their American father and an Italian mother. Their father had spent a lot of time teaching his children perfect English, and so, as a result, the siblings were bilingual, fluent in both languages.

Izzie ignored the staring eyes of the men as she strolled casually away from the boat. Her brother, who was directly behind her, was carrying their bags. She had her own carry-on satchel with the handle looped over her arm. She'd dressed like a lady, in her only fashionable dress, was wearing fancy gloves and a matching hat, and had dared to dab on just a tiny bit of lip color and rouge. She didn't need much. Her mother told her she was a natural beauty, and that was why everyone stared at her the way they did. She was trained to ignore it and never to put on airs because of it.

"You did nothing to create the beauty you have, Izzie dear," her mother had told her, "so do not take credit for it. Your beauty is due to God's design, and you should give thanks to the Creator, rather than taking credit when it is not yours to take."

"Yes, Mother," Izzie breathed aloud, her heart aching. She already missed her parents.

But it was time to venture out, and she knew it. She was twenty-four years old. She'd been longing to go to America for many years, and finally, her parents had agreed to it with one stipulation. She had to bring Lo along with her.

Izzie loved her brother and had no problem having him with her. He would keep her protected, her parents said, but Izzie knew it would be a two-way street. She would be protecting him as much as he was protecting her.

"Where will we go first?" Lo asked, sounding just like any American on the street. Izzie smiled at him.

"We will find a hotel to stay in. Do you have the money Papa gave to you?"

Lo set down one of the large trunks he was carrying and reached in his pocket, a look of inquiry on his face. He felt around in the pocket until his face lit up, and he withdrew a small folding wallet. "Yes. Here it is."

"Good. We may need to show our papers and pay fines. It will help us stay within the law of the country."

Lo's eyebrows pulled together, a worried look in his brown eyes. "But what law might we be breaking? We have broken no laws."

Izzie shook her head. "No, no, we have not. But just in case. We should keep as much of that as we can just in case we need it, yes?"

"Yes," Lo replied firmly, but she could tell he was still worried.

The new country provided many benefits and

opportunities for people from all around the world, Izzie's father had said. And he would not lie to his children. She was sure of that. Just like the land of milk and honey in the Bible, America would be the greatest land on earth. Izzie just knew it.

Bubbling with excitement, she gestured for Lo to pick up the luggage and follow her. He jumped into action, pocketing the folding wallet and grabbing the handle again. He was so eager. It made her feel even more energetic and anticipatory. Good things were going to happen.

Izzie spotted a newsstand and went in that direction, having to skirt around several people who were walking in a very determined manner. She halted in front of one to let him pass before she continued on her way.

Glancing over her shoulder to make sure her brother was still with her, Izzie ran her eyes over the offerings. There were three newspapers from neighboring towns and the *New York Times* on display. Of the magazines scattered across the rack, one caught her eye. She was drawn to the picture of a woman in a flowing pink dress and matching flowery hat. The woman was looking over her shoulder with a look of happiness plastered on her face. She was carrying a bouquet.

Izzie picked up the magazine and looked at it more closely. It was very thin. Just a few pages. She looked for a price. One penny. She had that. She had more than that.

"You can't just stand there looking at the pretty picture," she heard a gruff voice and lowered the magazine to see the round, sweating, sneering face of a dock worker—or more likely the newsstand worker. "I know ya cain't read it, so give it here."

Izzie frowned at the man, sharing a look with her brother. "I can read it fine. Thank you, sir," she said, making sure to speak in perfect dialect. "I will buy it." She pushed her fingers through the small coin purse dangling from her wrist and produced a shiny penny.

The man took it from her warily, examining it once it was in his hand as if he thought it might not be real.

Izzie tried to ignore the blatant bigotry. Her beauty didn't always win her friends. In fact, there were some who resented her, both men and women. She had learned to deal with each person individually and never held bad behavior against someone.

"Everyone is flawed," she heard her mother's voice in her ear. "You must always give the benefit of the doubt. They don't understand how rude they are.

Ignore them so you will always have peace in your heart knowing you are worthy of the best of everything."

Izzie turned away from the man, her eyes down on the magazine. The lessons she'd learned from her mother weren't exclusive to her. Lo had learned them all, too, even though he was not a great beauty like she was. He was a hard-working and good-looking young man, though. He would go far in life if he followed his mother's wise advice, which Izzie knew he planned to do.

"Let us find a good hotel, brother," she said softly, hurrying away from the newsstand and the busy dock filled with the hustle and bustle as dock-workers loaded and unloaded boats, going about their day doing their jobs.

"Yes, yes," Lo replied from behind her.

Izzie noticed how much quieter it was as they left the dock behind. There was a stretch of street where it was nothing but fields on both sides. It was quite a long walk to where the city began.

"This is pleasant," she remarked as they walked. "I am surprised there are not more people on this street."

"Others probably have horses and wagons and

things like that. They have ways to get around that we do not have."

Izzie accepted her brother's explanation with a nod. "No doubt you are correct," she stated.

A breeze lifted her brown hair from her shoulders. She closed her eyes briefly, enjoying it. It was strange how the smell of America was vastly different from her home in Italy. The scenery was much the same, as it looked like earth, with the ground and trees and buildings. But that was where the similarity stopped. She could tell she was going to have to get used to living in America.

5

Izzie walked into the hotel and went straight to the reception desk. She was anxious to get off her feet. The boat trip had been long, and her legs were weary from walking on solid ground.

"*Buongiorno,*" she greeted the young woman behind the counter. "I am looking for a room for my brother and me. That is, two rooms, if you please."

The girl gazed at Izzie. "All right, that's just fine." She turned the huge book that served as a log for guests around so that Izzie could sign in. "Please sign in for both of you. You would like two rooms, you say? Do you want them next to each other?"

Izzie wondered why she wouldn't want them next to each other. "*Si,* yes, please. With an adjoining door, if you have them."

"Yes, we do."

Izzie could tell by how the girl's eyes studied both her and Lo that it was obvious they weren't from America. She felt a little dismayed, as she wanted to fit in as much as possible. She'd bought a Western-style dress just for that purpose. But now that she was here, it seemed like the style she'd chosen wasn't a casual look. She wasn't sure what kind of impression she was giving off by wearing what she was wearing. Her father hadn't disapproved. Then again, he hadn't been in America in years.

After she'd signed in and paid for the two rooms, she and Lo went to the first one to talk.

"I'll stay in this one," she remarked as they went in, "and you take the other one."

"How long are we going to stay here?" Lo asked. "Do you have a plan for us?"

"I told you what the plan was before we left," Izzie replied, setting her fabric sack down on the bed. She pressed the mattress to see how firm it was. It was a little on the soft side, but she didn't mind. Hopefully, it wouldn't hurt her back. Soft mattresses tended to do that to her. She sat down and was satisfied with the bed right away. She crossed her legs and opened the magazine again, reading through the ads for a bride. "We will get jobs. Tomorrow we'll go out looking for a nice little house to rent. We might have to contend with a loft or rooms at a boarding house for now. We'll..."

She stopped talking, her eye catching on one of the ads. She closed the magazine on her finger and looked at the cover. It was a mail-order bride magazine, and she was just catching on to what it was used for. She truly had bought it for the cover.

"This magazine has advertisements for brides." She was astonished, and it came through in her voice.

"I beg your pardon?" Lo queried, his eyebrows shooting up. He dropped the luggage and came over to sit next to her on the bed, hovering over her shoulder to look.

"Men advertise for brides in this magazine," she explained, her voice a higher pitch than usual. "And look, there are two job advertisements here too."

Lo was quiet as he read the ads. "Those are for work. You should try one of the men. You've been wanting to get married anyway."

Izzie gasped, drawing back from Lo and giving him a questioning look. "Not like this. I wish to be married to a man who loves me. Not a man who advertised for me." She straightened herself and stared at the job advertisements on the last page. "I do want a job, though."

"But that's all the way in Texas."

Izzie chewed on her bottom lip. "They are willing to pay for someone to come and get married. I wonder if they will pay for someone to come and get a job."

"You are playing with fire, sister," Lo replied, moving to a chair near the nightstand. "You do not know those people. They might be dangerous."

Izzie laughed. "No matter where we go, there will be dangerous people. I would say it is probably safer to answer this ad and go to Texas to work than it would be to walk down these streets begging for a job. I do not want to starve. I will write to them now, and we will send the letter this afternoon."

"What am I going to do?" Lo asked curiously.

Izzie tilted her head to the side. "What do you mean?"

"When we go to Texas. What if they will not send money for a ticket for me? You cannot leave me here in New York."

Izzie had to let out another sharp laugh. Her

reply made her brother smile and blush, dropping his eyes to the floor. "Lorenzo Russo, I would never leave you behind. You will come with me if I have to hide you in a luggage trunk."

"I will not hide," Lo said, "I will ride beside you. I will pay my way."

"Do not worry yourself about it," Izzie replied. "We will always find a way to stay together. That is what Mama and Papa would want. Besides, if they found out I had left you behind, they would surely disown me."

Lo didn't disagree with her. He knew it was true just like she did. And she wouldn't ever even dream of doing anything without Lo, especially since they were in America. They were thousands of miles from home with a great body of water between them. She wasn't going to abandon her brother.

Since she was thinking about it, Izzie got up from the bed and turned around to rifle through her sack. She had the necessary tools to write letters, as she had been planning to write to her parents as often as possible. It wouldn't take long to compose a letter requesting employment and asking about the tickets. She made sure to mention how strong and capable Lo was. He would surely do well in Texas, where there were plenty of hard labor jobs that needed a strong, strapping young man like him.

She pictured the man on the receiving end of the employment request as an older gentleman with white hair and a neat, trim mustache that he would twitch with his lips while reading her letter.

When she was finished, she pulled out an envelope, tucked the letter inside, and sealed it.

"Let's go to the postmaster now," she said eagerly, tapping her brother's shoulder as she passed him heading to the door of her hotel room. He had slumped to the side, holding his head up with one fist, and was clearly almost asleep.

He jerked awake and shot to his feet.

"*Va bene...*" he said abruptly. "Yes, *si*, okay..."

She locked the door after they left, and the two hurried down the corridor to the concourse. There were more people in the lobby than there had been when they'd first arrived. She recognized several faces from the boat she'd been on. The sailors were staying at the hotel, too.

Izzie reached behind her and took Lo's hand, leading him through the small crowd to the front door. She didn't want to lose him. She could tell he was as intimidated by the group of men as she was.

"Come on, Lo," she murmured, tugging on his

hand. He nodded, saying nothing, following her out the door and down the street. She didn't know where the postmaster was, but she was determined to find it. Afterward, they would get a bite to eat.

She would make this a successful trip to America if it was the last thing she ever did.

6

―――――

It had been a successful morning. Luke was peacefully enjoying his lunch, the newspaper open in front of him. He'd come to Dylan's ranch for lunch because Mattie was an excellent cook and always made sure there was extra. She constantly had friends and family over. Everyone knew if they wanted something good to eat at a certain time of the day, they could stop in at the Sullivan ranch and eat to their heart's content.

They'd had a flood of advertisements for the next magazine edition. He was about as excited as he could get. They would have to reformat the layout since there were more articles and advertisements coming in than he'd expected.

When Harry Crowder, one of the boys who ran

around town distributing newspapers and magazines, came running around the side of Dylan's house, Luke sat forward anxiously. Harry would only have come to the ranch if there was a problem. And by the anxious look on his face, Luke could tell there was definitely a problem.

"What is it, Harry?" he asked, getting to his feet.

"Bobby…" the boy replied breathlessly. "Bobby tried to… to fix the… press, and… finger got… caught. He's… at the clinic."

"Good Lord, son," Luke cried out. He ran to the edge of the veranda and yelled out to Dylan, who was overseeing the finalization of his gazebo. Or Mattie's gazebo. "Dylan, Bobby got hurt. We gotta go to the clinic."

A worried look came to Dylan's face, and he hurried back toward the house. Luke had taken the stone steps down and met Dylan at the bottom. Dylan was looking at Harry, who had a frightened expression on his face.

"You look very distraught," he said urgently. "How bad is it? What happened? Is he alive?"

"He's alive, boss," Harry replied. "But he's got only them three fingers left now and his thumb. He was pokin' at something in the press, boss. And it moved and just cut it right off like that." He took one hand and sliced at his other hand with it like a karate chop. "Just like that, sir. And gone. It was on the floor. I saw it. There's lots of blood, too. All over the press machine."

The boy continued to speak breathlessly as they jogged around the house to the stables. Luke pictured their new press machine with blood all over it. The prospect of taking the machine apart to clean it and put it back together was a daunting one. Luke would almost rather beg Judge Holbrook for the money for a new one than have to clean the one soaked with blood.

"Too bad they can't just put his finger back on," Harry murmured, shaking his small head. "It was just cut clean off. Clean off." He sounded utterly amazed.

"I'll go to the clinic," Dylan said over Harry's head. "You go check out the machine and meet me at the clinic after. I want to know what shape it's in."

Luke knew his partner was also thinking about the clean-up expense. It wasn't something either he or Dylan had the knowledge to do. They could take anything apart to clean. But there was no way they would be able to put it back together correctly. Luke hadn't seen the inside mechanisms of a printing press in his entire life.

Once he was in the saddle, Luke didn't feel the need to stay with Dylan. He knew Harry would be right along with him as he rode quickly to the printing office.

He didn't separate from Dylan until they got into the heart of the busiest part of town. The clinic was up several streets, and the printing office was to the left much closer.

Luke left his horse out front of the building, glancing at the windows on either side of the front door before going through. He was surprised by what he saw. In the backroom, where both machines had been placed, he saw bodies moving around as people cleaned.

Relief flooded him as he went quickly to see who it was.

"I still see some right down there in that corner," he heard Mattie's voice and smiled.

"You can go on, Harry," Luke said, looking down at the boy. "Thanks for coming to get us. Really appreciate that. Take this for your trouble." He pulled a quarter from his pocket and handed it to the boy, whose eyes lit up at the sight of the money.

"Thanks, Mr. Turner," Harry cried out enthusiastically before bolting back to the front door and disappearing.

Mattie had heard Harry and stepped around the people scrubbing the blood from the wooden floor to come over to him.

"I guess Dylan must have gone to the clinic to see Bobby, huh?"

Luke nodded, glancing at her before moving his eyes around the room. "That is a lot of blood," he remarked, his surprise obvious in his voice. "Did he chop his hand off?"

Mattie shook her head, stepping back with him to examine the scene. "No. I wasn't here, but Penelope was, and she said it was his reaction that caused the amount. It was coming out a lot, she said anyway, squirting out, and he was flailing all over the place. Hence the blood on the windows and walls."

"Wow, poor fella," Luke murmured, shaking his head. Thinking about the accident made him flex his fingers, just to make sure they were all there. Mattie glanced at him and saw what he did as he crossed his arms in front of his chest.

"I did that, too," she observed. "It makes you feel like maybe it happened to you when you see this much blood."

Luke snorted. "I don't think I've ever seen this much blood before, so I have nothing to compare it to."

"All right, that's true," Mattie replied in an amused voice. "Do you think the machine will still work properly?"

Luke sighed. He didn't know, honestly, and had no idea what to tell her. What would her father think? Not even one edition into the magazine and the machine was already damaged or possibly damaged. Maybe it would just print in red for a while.

The thought was both amusing and disgusting at the same time.

"I hope so," he said. "I don't want your pa to think his money went to waste on this machine."

"He won't think that," she responded firmly and quickly. "That's not my father, and you know it. He will likely offer to help out Bobby's family for a while until they figure out what they're going to do."

"Bobby can come back when he recovers," Luke stated, looking down at her. "He can train himself to do this job with a finger missing. It doesn't take every one of your fingers to do what he does."

Mattie nodded with a look of satisfaction on her slender face. "You're right. And nothing happened to his brain, huh?"

"Right."

They were quiet for a moment before she said, "Do you think that's what Dylan is telling him now?"

"Probably," Luke replied with some confidence. He and Dylan were often on the same wavelength. He had no doubt Dylan was as sympathetic to Bobby as he would have been, even though there was no reason the accident should have happened. He had to have done something wrong. It was his error that would have caused him to lose a finger.

Luke would never say that to the young man. It was a shame someone of only twenty-five years of age would be mutilated so early in life. But at least he was alive. That was all that really mattered.

7

Dylan was, in fact, doing just that. After Luke got an eyeful of what was going on at the printing office, he went to the clinic just to make sure. He didn't expect to find Dylan berating Bobby or swearing at him. He expected just what he walked into.

Bobby was sitting on an examination bed in one of the two rooms in the clinic. Dylan was standing near the door and looked over at Luke when he came in. The two men nodded at each other in greeting.

"You all right?" Luke asked, going over to bend at the waist and stare mercilessly at Bobby's bandaged hand. It was very obvious that his index finger was completely gone. It looked like it had been severed right at the knuckle. Luke didn't want to know how that happened.

"I will be," Bobby responded in a groggy voice. Luke looked into the young man's eyes and saw he was half out of it. Luke didn't smell alcohol, so it must have been some kind of medication the doctor put Bobby on to help with the pain.

"You get some morphine?" he asked.

"Yeah," Dylan answered for Bobby, who just nodded and swayed on the edge of the bed.

"Maybe you should lay back," Luke remarked, taking hold of Bobby's shoulder and directing the man back on the bed, "before you fall."

"I wanna go back to work," Bobby mumbled, even though he was now stretched out on the bed, his head back, his eyes closed. "I need... to... go..." His voice trailed off, and the next moment, they heard him snoring.

"Let's get out of here," Dylan said, jerking his head toward the door. "Let him get some sleep. Poor kid. I can't believe he did this to himself."

"What was he doing that made that happen?" Luke asked, not sure he really wanted to know. They left the room behind and then left the clinic together.

"He told me he saw something inside the mechanism. Or something fell down in there. A paper clip, maybe. I don't know exactly. He was trying to poke it out. At first, he used a pencil. He got whatever it was closer and then put his finger in to jog it out. He must have bumped the machine because one of the levers came down and went right through his finger."

A flash of pain went through Luke as he imagined that event. "That poor kid," he repeated Dylan's phrase. "I don't even want to think about it. You told him he still has a job when he recovers, right?"

Dylan gave Luke a narrow look. "Of course I did. He doesn't need all his fingers to work for us. And if he did, I'd find another job for him. He can't live and support his family without a job."

"Agreed," Luke said, nodding firmly.

"Mr. Turner."

Luke turned when a young voice called out his name.

"Mr. Sullivan."

The young man running toward them waved several envelopes over his head. "You got more mail, Mr. Turner, Mr. Sullivan. Probably for your magazine, huh?"

Luke smiled at Andrew. "I'm sure they are, Andrew. You know we aren't that popular ourselves."

Andrew laughed heartily, shaking his head. "Oh, Mr. Turner. I'm sure that ain't true. Here ya go."

He handed them the envelopes and, without waiting for a tip, turned and darted back toward the postmaster's office.

"Hey, Andrew," Luke called out, hurriedly pulling a quarter from his pocket. The ten-year-old spun around but continued to run backward a few paces. Luke flipped the coin through the air with his thumb.

Andrew reacted with delight, jumping up in the air and catching the quarter. He beamed at Luke.

"Thank you."

Luke waved at him as he ran off again. "You're welcome," he called out. He turned his grin to Dylan, who had his head tilted and was looking at the envelopes in Luke's hands. "Great kid."

Dylan nodded. "Yeah, he is. Give me a couple of those, would ya?"

He held out a hand, a curious look on his face. Luke gave him three of the six envelopes, and the two men began walking again as they examined the correspondence.

Luke's three envelopes were all of a different variety. The one on the top was from a man wishing to place an ad. He could tell by the return name. The second letter had a female name in return, and the third didn't have a return name at all, just a hotel name in New York.

Curious about the no-name envelope, Luke tucked the other two under his arm and slid his finger through the flap of the envelope.

The paper he withdrew from the envelope was different. It was unlike any other paper he'd received so far. The corners were jagged on all sides as if cut by an uneven pair of scissors. It was thicker than normal paper and had a grainy feel to it, instead of being smooth like other paper.

He smelled a scent drifting from it that was unlike anything he'd smelled before. There was something special about this letter, he decided. If it was from a female wanting companionship, he would be responding to it in a hurry.

"This is interesting," he remarked, reading through the letter. It had a friendly tone but, unfortunately, was not from a lady who wished to become a bride. This woman wanted to work in the office as the receptionist. Luke had been considering Penelope for the job, but she was not as reliable as Luke would like. She had other responsibilities.

"What is it?" Dylan asked, looking up from his letters.

"This young woman wants the receptionist job," Luke said, reading the words written in elegant cursive handwriting. Whoever had trained this woman to write did a wonderful job. "It looks like she can certainly read, write, and spell. Sounds highly educated."

"You sound surprised," Dylan remarked, his own voice expressing his bewilderment. "There are a lot of women who know how to read and write just as well as us."

Luke nodded. "I know. Her name is Isabella Russo. She just came from Italy with her brother Lorenzo, and they are looking for jobs." He looked up at Dylan. "I bet you could put her brother to work on your ranch."

Dylan nodded, interest in his eyes. "I could, yes. Still don't know why you're so surprised."

"Well, they're obviously Italian. Nice that they know how to read and write English. And look at this handwriting." He turned the paper around and showed Dylan. He was highly impressed with the woman, and he hadn't even met her yet. "I bet she's real classy. Dignified. Probably raised by scholars and wealthy parents."

"Must have been if they could afford to send her to America."

"And her brother, too," Luke added.

"Yeah, that, too. So write to her."

"She wants to know if we can send her two tickets, one for her and one for her brother."

Dylan nodded, much to Luke's relief. He would have sent the tickets without Dylan's approval, but it was much nicer when he had it.

"I'll send it right out to them, then," he replied with a return nod. "I'm gonna write that and send it out now. Go by the train station and arrange a couple of tickets. What are you gonna do this afternoon?"

"I'm going to the printing office. I need to see about that machine."

"Well, you know more about those things than I do. I hope it works without a problem. I know I can't fix it."

"I'll take a look," Dylan said. "Meet up with you later on."

"Okay, that sounds good."

The tone of the letter and the uniqueness of the paper stayed on Luke's mind for the rest of the day. He wished there was a way to get the Italian woman and her brother there right then. But he would have to be patient. He had no other choice.

8

Izzie scrubbed the floor vigorously, using all her energy to get a spot left by a boot heel from the polished tiles. It had been two weeks since she sent her letter to Texas, and she was hoping a return letter would come any day now. She knew it could take another week but prayed every day the mail carriers would have wings on their feet.

She and Lorenzo had managed to get temporary cleaning positions at the church across the street from the hotel where they were still staying. The cost was the same as the boarding house, and they'd gotten comfortable in the two rooms they were offered. The price came with three square meals a day and the opportunity to take a bath twice a week.

Izzie sat back on her haunches and surveyed her

work, placing her wet hands on her wet apron pressed against her wet dress. She would be glad to get up off the floor and into some dry clothes at the end of her workday.

"Oh, Miss Isabella." The vicar of the church rushed toward her, holding out both hands. "You must get up off the floor. Look at you. There is no need to exert yourself so exuberantly. The floor will still be there tomorrow, and people will still walk on it, as they always do."

Izzie took one of the man's hands and used his strength to pull herself to her feet. She did feel grungy and dirty in her wet clothes, clutching a large sponge in one hand. She wiped her forehead with the back of the other one, shaking her head. "I am sorry, Vicar, I do not believe I can remove that stain. Someone has truly put their heel down right there." She was a bit disappointed in herself. Normally, she was very good at cleaning.

"You do a wonderful job, Miss Isabella," he replied, shaking his head. He had let her hand go but had rested his hand on her arm instead. "You and your brother are very hard workers. I'm sure you'll do wonderfully in Texas. And you don't appear to eat much, so you will make a lot of money to put aside." The vicar laughed delightedly at his own joke.

Isabella grinned warmly. "Yes, that is very true." She laughed, too, though she wasn't sure why it was funny.

"You go on and get changed, dear. I'll tell Lorenzo he can go, too. I will give him a dollar bonus, and you two should go get something good to eat for dinner." He winked at her. "I know the hotel food is good, but the restaurant... well, their food is better, I must say."

Isabella let out a pleasant laugh. "You are so kind to us, Vicar. *Grazie mille*. Thank you so much."

"*Prego*," the vicar responded.

Isabella giggled and put one hand over her mouth, saying, "Oh." in a high-pitched tone. "You have learned an Italian word. You are very precious, Vicar. Very precious." She patted him on the arm and turned to leave. He was a kind man, offering them a helping hand the first Sunday they came to visit the church. Neither she nor Lo was surprised that he needed help. They were more surprised that he didn't already have it. He was an older man with shaggy white hair and a slender body bordering on just a little too thin. They'd spent the first week just dusting, cleaning the surfaces, washing the windows of the church and the parish.

Isabella didn't mind the job, but she dreamed of being in Texas, behind the desk in a printing press office, listening to the whirring of the machine in the back, making magazines with pretty pictures. She was sure *Bridal Bliss* would bring much happiness to a great many lonely people. She wanted to be a part of that. She wanted to help make people happy and bring couples together to love each other all their lives.

And Lo was right. Maybe she would find love herself. It could happen.

Isabella was smiling as she silently stripped off her wet clothes and replaced them with clean, dry clothes. She chose a green dress that was a style typically worn in Italy but not seen as much on the streets of New York. She wasn't interested in drawing attention to herself, so she covered the dress with a large shapeless cloak. She couldn't do anything about the obvious beauty of her face. That would automatically draw attention whether she was dressed in a beautiful gown or a burlap sack.

She vowed to keep her head down and not look at anyone other than her brother and the serving girl at the restaurant.

When Isabella was dressed, she crossed the room to stand at the window and look out at the busy street of New York outside. There were many people walking up and down the sidewalk. She could hear vendors calling out their wares for customers to buy. Children ran up and down and around, chasing balls and hoops and each other. She'd even seen a motorcar, what was the first one in America, she was told, being driven up the street past her hotel. She wasn't the only one staring as it went past. The street was lined with people on both sides. Some of them threw bits of paper in the air, and there were many cheers as it went by. The man driving it waved, his smile beaming as bright as the sun.

She looked toward the entrance of the hotel and saw her brother running toward the door. He disappeared from her vision, and she waited for him to come knocking on her door.

"Izzie," he called out while still in the hallway. Her door was flung open a second later, and he came bursting through, his eyes wide and excited. "Look. He gave me a dollar so we could get something to eat."

"I know," she replied, smiling at him. "He told me he was going to."

"Well, let us go now. I am going to starve. It has been so long since I have last eaten."

Isabella laughed, her affection for her brother coursing through her veins. "Oh, you. It has only been since this afternoon for lunch. I found the vicar's sandwiches to be quite satisfying."

"*Si*, you would, *mia sorella*, but I am still a growing man, and I need much more nourishment than simple sandwiches."

They both laughed. He stopped abruptly and ran his eyes over her from head to toe.

"Why is it that you wear such clothes?" he asked, sweeping his hand up and down her body. "You hide what is beautiful underneath this sack cloth?"

"*Grazie*, brother, but I do not wish to draw attention to myself."

"No, no, Izzie, you do not hide yourself. You must be proud of yourself. Not ashamed."

Isabella shook her head, but she was already unbuttoning the tent-like coat. "I am not ashamed, Lo. I fear it will bring us attention we do not want. You will protect me at all costs, and I do not wish to see you harmed. The men here are not as nice as they are in Italy."

Lo narrowed his eyes. "There are nice men here and nice men there. There are evil men here and evil men there. They will be there wherever you go, Izzie. You must not hide yourself in fear. We will not let anything happen to you. We will work together as a team, and you will be safe. *Si?*"

Isabella tilted her head and gave him an affectionate look. "*Si, mio fratello.*"

She shrugged off the coat and walked to him. He put his arm around her shoulders, and the two left the room with their heads held high.

9

Isabella and Lorenzo had the next day off, and the plan was to sleep in.

That plan was ruined in the early hours of the morning when the sun had just come up, and the town began to wake up. There were some men up earlier than everyone else. They had apparently been roaming the streets, looking for trouble.

Isabella herself might have slept through the ruckus, and she did, for the initial start of the riot. But she had no choice but to wake up when her brother began shaking her shoulders.

"Izzie," he was hissing in a frantic voice. "You must wake up. We must get out of here."

Isabella shook her head to clear it, sitting up in bed. The loud sounds outside her window helped to bring her to full alertness. Her eyes widened and swiveled to her brother.

"What is this? What is going on?" Without waiting for him to answer, she slid from her bed and hurried to the window, clutching her nightgown in her hands anxiously. She had only glanced through the glass when she pulled back suddenly as a bottle flew past the window.

She moved close again and looked out.

There was one group of men standing on one side of the street and another group of men on the opposing side. The crowds were made up mostly of men, but several tough-looking women were in the group, as well.

"What are they fighting about?" Isabella asked, her heart pounding a mile a minute.

"Some of them are saying bad things about foreigners. I think we should leave, Izzie. Now."

"But we are still waiting for the letter from Texas. What if we do not receive the letter. We cannot go now."

Lo's face collapsed in anger, and he stalked over to the window to stand beside her. He took her arm in a painfully tight grip and jerked her slightly toward the window. "Look at what you see out there, Izzie. They are knocking on doors. They are going to come here soon. I am surprised they have not come already. Is this not where foreigners go when traveling?"

Isabella knew her brother was right. Fear pierced her, though she did not want it. She was a strong woman, an independent woman.

But she was also a smart woman. And she knew that neither her strength nor her confidence would matter to those men out there.

She nodded. "You are right, *mio fratello*. Let us pack our things and go. We will stop by the postmaster's and see if there is a letter for us. If there is, we will know this is God's will."

"*Si.*" Without another word, Lo disappeared into the room adjoining hers. Moments later, he reappeared with his luggage trunk in hand. He gave her a sheepish grin that showed his fear. "I may have thrown everything in my trunk before I came to get you up. I will be honest, I thought you would already be awake and also getting your things together."

It didn't take long for Isabella to do just that. Less than five minutes later, the siblings were out in the hallway, looking to the left and right, trying to decide the best way to get out without being seen.

They were given their answer when the front door of the hotel down the stairs to their right burst open. They heard stomping boots, yelling voices, and breaking glass. Isabella didn't want to know what they were breaking or why they would vandalize the hotel. The owner was not responsible for their prejudice.

Gathering all her courage, Isabella grabbed her brother's arm, as both his hands were taken up with their luggage, and pulled him down the hallway to the left. Her heart raced as fear slid through her. She was trembling like a leaf, trying to hide it from Lo as best she could.

They reached the door at the end of the hall, and Isabella grabbed the handle, shoving it down and pushing. She was momentarily terrified when the door didn't seem to want to move. She put a little more effort into it, and it popped open, sending her out the door with more force than she'd intended. She caught herself, though, and regained her balance. Lo shot out the door behind her, turned, and shoved it closed, not caring if it slammed and made a loud noise.

The siblings were standing on the outdoor landing of a set of stairs going down to the ground. Isabella waited for him to go down first because he didn't have a free hand, and if he tripped, she would see and be able to grab him from behind.

They both made it to the ground without trouble, spinning in a u-turn to go to the back alleyway, away from the raging crowd in the main street.

"I want to get out of here, Izzie," Lo said, his voice sounding much younger than usual. When she looked at him, she saw the fear in his eyes. It reminded her of when he was on the schoolyard with her and other boys were teasing him.

"We are, Lo," she replied, forcing her voice to sound confident. "We're going to make it. Don't worry. Come on. Let's hurry."

She pulled him down the alley to the back road, and they took off on foot, running as fast as they could, away from the rioting in the street.

Isabella's heart didn't slow down until they were in front of the postmaster's office. It was still early, and he had not arrived to open up yet. They were far enough away from the hotel and the danger for Isabella to calmly stand outside and wait. She kept her eyes on the distance, though, hopeful that they wouldn't bring their anger and bitterness that far down the road.

"Well, good morning, there, you two."

She turned swiftly, her heart hammering for a moment, even though the voice was friendly.

"Come to check for some mail, have you?" It was

the postmaster, a man named Edwin Cox. He had been very friendly to them since they'd arrived in New York. Isabella wanted to think of him as a friend, but her father had warned her not to jump to the conclusion that everyone that was nice to her was her friend. He cautioned her to take her time making decisions about people because her beauty and independence would cause some to lie to her, use her, deceive her.

She wanted to be friendly, but she did not want to be hurt. She gave the man a pleasant smile.

"Yes, we are anxious to receive a letter, and we are hoping it is here today."

His voice was doubtful when he answered, but Isabella chose not to hear it.

"We did get a shipment in this morning. I will certainly check it for your letter."

The siblings followed the tall man into the little building. A large sack was placed on a table behind the long counter. Tingles ran up Isabella's arms when she saw it.

The letter she was hoping for had to be in there. It had to be.

Her brother must have been thinking the same thing. She felt him grab at her hand, and she let him take it, glancing over at him, noticing his excited eyes.

Once inside, she set her traveling bag on a table nearby. Edwin hurried to the bag. He looked at them before turning the bag over and dumping out the contents. There were more letters than Isabella had hoped for.

But he sorted through them quicker than she expected he would, probably because he was used to doing it, and soon held up a letter in the air, a big smile on his face.

"I believe this is for you." He looked at the front of the envelope. "Isabella Russo?"

She could barely contain her excitement. "That is me," she exclaimed.

She hurried to him and took the letter from his hands, staring down at it.

"This is it, sister," Lo said quietly behind her. "Open it."

10
___

The scenery passed quickly, but Isabella could still see the beauty of it all. She was seated in the window seat on the train while her brother took the aisle seat so he could stretch his legs out into the space between. He made sure to pull them back whenever someone came walking along.

He was resting, his eyes closed, his head back on the seat behind him. Other than the sound of the wheels churning on the tracks and an occasional whistle from the engine, there was no sound. All Isabella had was her thoughts.

She had bought a book at the train station so she would have something to do on the long train ride to

Texas. But she was too excited to read it and too excited to sleep like Lo was.

So she sat back in her chair, watching the trees rush by, fascinated by the sculpted mountains in the distance. She was going to Texas.

Texas.

She and Lo were about to start a new life. She pictured herself sitting behind a desk, smiling at people coming in, filing papers as ads came in for the magazine. She was so excited she didn't know how to handle it. Her smile was permanent.

A tug on her chair made Isabella sit forward and look over her shoulder. A little girl was behind her, in the chair that was facing the other direction with its back to hers. The little girl's eyes widened, and she dropped down so she couldn't be seen. Isabella's eyes met with the man across the space from the little girl, sitting in the chair facing her.

"I apologize if she's bothering you," the man said, his dark brown mustache twitching with amusement. He was obviously not bothered by the child. The twinkle in his eye made Isabella smile, and she shook her head in response.

"She is not bothering me, sir. She is quite a beautiful little girl. Is she yours?"

"Why yes, she is. You don't see the resemblance?"

He took his hat off and held it to the side, giving Isabella the silliest smile he could manage.

She laughed softly. "Ah, yes, I see it now."

"You are silly, Papa." The little girl laughed as she threw herself into her father's arms, climbing up on his lap to wrap her arms around his neck. She gave him repeated kisses on the cheek while he squinted and pretended to try to push her away from him. He was actually holding onto her tightly as he "pushed" her away.

"Where are you going?" Isabella asked. She reacted when Lo tugged on her sleeve, making her look at him. He was shaking his head.

"That is a personal question, Izzie," he hissed softly.

"We're going all the way to California," the man answered, apparently not hearing Lo or noticing he was lightly scolding his sister. He was looking at his daughter, his grin still plastered to his face. "And we're going to have a wonderful time in the warm weather, aren't we, darling?"

"Yes, Papa. We are."

The girl bopped his nose and laughed like it was the funniest thing she had ever done.

"This is my little girl, Rose," the man said. "I am

Winston Campbell. You are not from America, are you?"

Isabella shook her head. "No, my brother and I are from Italy, a little village called Portofino. I'm sure you've never heard of it."

Mr. Campbell shook his head. "No, I'm afraid not. I don't do much traveling overseas. I don't do any traveling overseas, as a matter of fact." He laughed. "You speak remarkably good English. Did you go to school here?"

"No, my father taught me English, to read and write, also. And my brother, too." Isabella gave Lo an affectionate smile, which he returned. "He was American, living abroad. He married my mother and stayed in Italy to raise us. Now that we are grown, he has given us the means to travel to America and see what all the fuss is about."

Talking to the stranger was the first instance she'd felt unsure of her English and hesitated to make sure she got the right word. They had only ever spoken English to a handful of people in Italy other than her father. Slang words weren't something her father often used, so she had to make sure she was saying it right. She didn't want to look like a fool.

Mr. Campbell responded by putting his daughter

on the seat next to him and patting her on the head. "Well, the fuss for us is in California, isn't that right, darling?"

"Yes, Papa." The girl cried vehemently, immediately getting to her feet on the chair and leaning back to wrap her arms around it behind her. She bobbed her knees and bounced in place, grinning at Isabella.

"And where are you headed?" Mr. Campbell asked.

"We are going to Texas. I have been offered a job there. As a receptionist."

She beamed at him proudly. She couldn't help it. It felt like almost the moment she got off the boat, things went the way she wanted them to. She couldn't ask for more than that, could she?

"I bet you are really excited, aren't you?" the man asked, studying her face.

Isabella nodded. The stranger had no idea just how excited she really was—the thought of the sunshine, so much warmer and drier than New York. The only thing she had qualms about was the behavior of the men. She'd heard stories about cowboys in the wild west. But the men in New York were no less violent, in her opinion, and the fact that they were all so close together, instead of being spread apart like in the west, made it even more volatile.

"We *are* excited," Lo said while she was wrapped in her thoughts. "And I have decided that I want to be called Dusty instead of Lorenzo." He grinned from ear to ear. "Do you think this will make me more American?"

Mr. Campbell laughed and looked at his daughter. "I think he looks like Dusty. What do you think, darling?"

"Yes, Papa," the little girl cried, clapping her hands together and bouncing on the seat.

Laughing some more, her father shook his head, returning his eyes to Isabella and Lo. "Sometimes I wonder if that's all she can say. She's such an agreeable little doll, aren't y..." He cut himself off, averting his eyes to Isabella only long enough to wink at her. "Aren't you, darling?"

The child laughed heartily. "Oh yes, Papa."

This caused all of them to laugh along with her. Isabella's heart was filled with happiness and hopefulness. She was having a wonderful time on the train ride to her new life and prayed it was a sign that she was meant to be going where she was going.

She and Lo would prosper in Texas, she just knew it. She couldn't wait to write to her mother and father and tell them their adventures had already begun. She knew they would be delighted to hear that their children had not gotten conventional cleaning and labor jobs, planting themselves in New York. They would be in the west, where the country could be seen just by stepping outside the door.

Luke leaned against the outer wall of the train station, watching for it to pull in. He'd been waiting anxiously for it to arrive. It was normally a busy day for him at the press. The magazine was in full swing, and he desperately needed Isabella's help. He hoped she would fit right in and not need much training.

He was apprehensive about getting her all the way from New York, but her letter had been so impressive. He could tell she was highly intelligent, and that's just what he was looking for.

He heard the train before he saw it barreling down the tracks toward them. He pushed himself from his relaxed position and joined several other people at the end of the platform so they would be there when their expected visitors stepped off.

Luke moved his head and his eyes with the train as it went past him. It was slow enough for him to see the faces of the people in the windows. He spotted several young women with young men but had no way of knowing which couple was Isabella and Lorenzo.

He had to take a step back when there was a surge of people toward the stopped train. He swerved his head from left to right, looking for two Italians.

When Isabella got off the train, he knew exactly who she was. There was no mistaking the foreign beauty. Luke had never seen a woman so beautiful in his entire life. He exercised self-control immediately, knowing that she probably got that same reaction from 90% of the men she met. He didn't want to be like all the others. He had hired her for a job, and that's what she was going to do, despite her extreme beauty.

He stepped over to them, looking up at her brother as he followed her out of the train. He had similar looks, but while her eyes were brown, his eyes were hazel and light-colored, in contrast to his darker skin and hair color.

The best thing about the two of them was that they were smiling when they saw him approaching. From that initial sight, he took it that neither of them was particularly unhappy about leaving Italy. They were both excited to be in America and were happy to be on such a grand adventure. She had said as much in her letter but seeing their delighted faces for the first time made it a fact in his mind.

"Hello," he said, lifting one hand and waving it to get their attention. "Over here. You must be Isabella and Lorenzo."

He leaned forward to shake Lorenzo's hand first, as he was the man, after all.

"I wish to be called Dusty from now on," Lorenzo said in a bright, spirited voice.

Isabella laughed. "I am telling you, Lorenzo, you will not get used to that."

"But if everyone thinks that is my name, I will have to get used to it, will I not?"

Luke was thrilled with them both right away. He lifted both arms outstretched as if he was about to go in for a group hug but instead stood still, saying, "Let us go to the buggy. I'll take you to the house you'll be staying in. If you are hungry, that is the best place to grab yourself something to fill those tummies. Then I'll take you to the press, where you will be working,

Isabella." He pressed his hands flat together in front of him and bowed slightly at the waist, keeping his eyes on her and gesturing slightly toward her with his hands.

"Please, call me Izzy. It is not a new name, and it is one that I will recognize." She gave her brother a teasing look, which endeared her to Luke even more.

"Izzy it is, then. Of course I am Luke Turner, and you can both call me Luke." He gave Lorenzo a friendly look. "You, my young friend, will be working at the ranch, the Sullivan ranch, owned by my dear friend and business partner, Dylan. And I'm afraid we already have a Dusty working for us, believe it or not."

Lorenzo looked disappointed, but his face brightened when he said, "Then you must call me Lorenzo. Or Lo. I can think of no other name that does not sound Italian. Lo does not sound like anything, does it?" He laughed.

"No, I reckon it doesn't. If y'all will follow me, I'll take you to my buggy, and we'll get on out of here."

"Don't forget our luggage," Isabella said urgently, resting her hand against his arm as he turned away. He looked down at it, thinking how smooth and soft her hand was. She jerked it away, coloring in her cheeks prettily.

"I am sorry," he rushed to say. "I almost forgot, didn't I? I guess I'm in a hurry to show you everything. I've never been able to give a tour of my home and business before. I think this will be fun. And very interesting."

As they went to the station building and Lo went in with their tickets to collect their bags, Isabella gave him an intrigued look.

"How is it interesting?" she asked curiously.

"I would like to know what my life looks like from the outside, from a stranger's point of view. This house that I'm taking you to is where Dylan and I used to live before he got married and bought his ranch. The one Lo will be working at."

Isabella nodded. "I see," she said softly. He could tell she did see. She did understand what he was saying. It made him want to keep talking.

"I always tried to keep the place nice and tidy. Now that Dylan's been gone for a while, it seems a lot bigger than it was because it's always neat and tidy. He's not neat and tidy." He said the last words almost under his breath, which made his companions laugh.

Lo came out, and they all headed toward the end of the platform, where four steps down would take them to the lot where the buggy sat amongst others.

He helped Isabella in the front passenger seat of the buggy while Lo climbed in the back. He circled around and got in himself, taking the reins in one hand. Glancing over his shoulder at Lo, he asked, "Do you know how to drive a team of horses?"

"Yes, definitely," Lo answered, nodding vigorously.

"Good." Luke nodded. "That's always helpful. I take it you know how to shoot a gun and ride a horse, as well."

"Yes, I can do both things," Lo answered. "And Izzie is also proficient in those things."

Luke smiled at her. He really thought he'd done a good job not letting her beauty distract him from what he had planned to say to them upon their arrival. He found that not looking directly at her helped a lot. When he did, he was washed over with a feeling of warmth, taken in by the depth of her brown eyes, the smoothness of her skin, the shapely form of her face, and her figure.

Luke had to pull himself out of the reverie, realizing he had let himself think too deeply about the subject. He had to stay focused. It was a good thing he had an office. He could close the door, so he didn't have to stare at her beautiful face all day long.

Luke commanded himself to calm down and

collect his thoughts. He was a decent, hard-working man. Yes, he might have been having thoughts lately of finding a bride but even as a receptionist, Isabella was out of his league. She was too beautiful for words.

That was probably why she was unattached. She was smart, which meant she would be able to tell when a man was having her on. She could probably see through falsehoods and fables faster than the person speaking them.

He would have to be careful to make sure he spoke to her with respect at all times.

And make sure everyone else did, too.

12

———

Isabella was absolutely thrilled to see Luke when she got off the train. Sitting beside him in the buggy made her feel strange. It was a feeling she had never had before. If she had to put a label on it, she would call it insecurity. No man had ever made her feel insecure before.

Luke Turner had a presence about him. He was obviously a physically strong man, broad-shouldered and muscled. But it wasn't just that. He gave off a vibe—a feeling that nearly overwhelmed Isabella.

She reminded herself she was about to be his employee. He was providing a place for her and her brother to live while they worked for him and his business partner. He was giving her more than any stranger was required to give another stranger. Much, much more.

Isabella already knew how to show respect to those in authority over her. Her father had trained her in the art of being a woman in a man's world. He'd done a surprisingly effective job, considering he had never been a woman in a man's world. He gave her insight into the way men thought and tips on how to deal with the chauvinistic men, of whom there were many.

Luke was definitely not one of them. Isabella could tell. She was relieved and knew her father would be when he read her letters to him. She planned to write one that very night and would write as many as she could until he begged her to stop.

The thought of her father begging her to stop writing to him flooded Isabella with emotion. She missed him. She missed her mother.

With a mist of tears in her eyes, she glanced over her shoulder at Lo. He was leaning out the side of the buggy, looking at the scenery as they passed it with wide, excited eyes. He must have sensed he was being looked at because he turned to meet her eyes with his own.

The moment between them brought Isabella's

tears to the surface. She reached back and took his hand, remembering the fear she'd felt when they felt threatened at the hotel. She could vaguely still hear the sound of the slurs those men were hurling at each other. The strangest thing was that neither party was truly American. They were two sides of immigrants who brought their battle from their native countries to the soil of America.

Isabella shrugged off the memory when her brother squeezed her hand and smiled at her.

"We're gonna be okay, Izzie," he said comfortingly. "I promise you, we're gonna be okay. Mr. Turner isn't gonna let us get hurt." He turned hopeful eyes to the back of Luke's head. He couldn't very well turn his head all the way around, so he looked at Isabella with a warm smile and nodded.

"He's right. I won't let anything happen to you. You don't have to worry anyway. Bighorn is probably a lot more massive and has a lot more people than you're used to. But I promise you, most of them are good people, not just at heart but out in the open, too. They'll help you if you need help. And they won't hurt you for no reason."

"Do you have riots in your streets?" Isabella asked, thinking it was an innocent question.

Luke reacted by lifting his eyebrows and

widening his eyes. "Riots? In the streets? Here? No, ma'am. You won't find any of that here. Did you see one in New York?"

Isabella nodded. She was a little taken aback by how surprised he was. She thought everyone knew the difference between the two parts of the country.

"Life is very different there," she remarked.

"But you were only there a couple of weeks, right? Didn't you write to me right after you got off the boat?"

"Yes, quite quickly, in fact," she affirmed.

"Well, you don't have to worry about that here. I promise. We see very little action around here. The most you'll see is a saloon brawl that might spill out in the streets. But that's it."

"There are a lot more people there." Isabella's voice was soft when she made her observation. Her eyes were turned to the sides of the street, where people were walking along the sidewalk, talking. Children ran in front of the buggy and disappeared quickly enough in an alleyway on the other side.

"I like it here already," Lo said from the back seat. Isabella glanced back at him, smiling. It made her heart happy to see him grinning the way he was, his eyes flashing with excitement.

"There's the press right there," Luke said as they

passed a small two-story building with a large window in the front. The words "Sullivan/Turner Press" were painted on the window in bright white and yellow letters. "We'll come back after you get settled in at the house. I want you to be able to refresh yourselves if you like.

"Thank you, Luke," Isabella said in a warm voice. "You are very considerate."

The look he gave her suggested he didn't know how to take that compliment. His eyes were only on her for a second before he looked at the road in front of them again.

Isabella was once again amazed by the sight of the house they would be staying in. There was yard space on all four sides, with more in the back and the front. The home itself was two stories with what was probably an attic with a widow walk.

The house had a wrap-around porch and six steps to ascend to go in the front door. The entire house was a dull yellow color. Isabella thought the choice of using bright canary-yellow shutters made it look like a wilted sunflower.

"This is beautiful," she murmured.

Luke gave her an intense look she didn't understand before saying, "Thank you. I would take the credit, but I bought it like this."

She giggled at his joke as she got down from the buggy. The two men pulled out the luggage trunks and followed behind her as she went up the steps.

She looked over her shoulder at Luke. "Should I just go in? Is it locked?"

"No, it's not locked. I think the housekeeper might be in there right now, actually. Dylan would be at his ranch. We'll go see him after we stop at the press. You can meet the people we have working there."

"Sounds wonderful." Isabella turned back to the door and pulled open the screen first before turning the knob and pushing the door open on the inside.

She stepped back and held the screen so the two men could pass in front of her. They both gave her regretful looks, and she knew it was because she was holding the door for them instead of the other way around. She went after them inside and stopped abruptly to look around. The foyer was a decent size. The floor was clean and shiny. There were stairs to her right, going up to the second floor. There was a door before the staircase. It was open, and through it, she could see the furnishings of a living room or parlor.

"That's where we spend most of our free time..." Luke shook his head, chuckling. "We used to anyway. I reckon when he comes to visit, we still spend the majority of our time in there. The rest of the time would be in the dining room. Dylan does like to eat."

Isabella could tell Luke was used to having his business partner with him all the time. He'd mentioned him more than a handful of times since picking them up at the train station.

"We will be meeting this Dylan Sullivan, won't we?"

"You will, yes," Luke nodded.

"Good." She gave him a return nod. "It will be nice to put a name to a face."

13

———

The press was just as impressive as the house. Isabella and Lo were too anxious and excited to eat, so as soon as they got a quick tour of the house and settled their bags in their rooms, they asked to be taken to the press. Isabella was really the one pushing to go. She wanted to see her office—if she had one— or at least her desk.

Penelope Greenwood was the other worker in the office. She was a haggard-looking, thin woman probably in her mid-forties with sharp eyes unhidden behind large glasses that sat like saucers on her face. She was spritely and quick when she moved, reminding Isabella of a mouse.

Despite her somewhat odd appearance, Penelope was friendly and had a kind voice. Her smile completely transformed her face and brought out good feelings in Isabella.

She got a chance to sit at her desk and scan the press room that had recently been cleaned thoroughly. She heard what had happened to the young man working before she came. He was still recovering at home, but apparently, Penelope expected he would return soon.

After a bit of small talk, Luke asked the siblings if they were hungry yet.

Isabella looked at her brother. She could eat but wasn't particularly hungry. He raised his eyebrows and shrugged.

"I do not think there is a need to stop here in town. We are going to the ranch, yes? We can get something there if your business partner allows it. I am not yet very hungry, and I do not believe Lo is either." She gave him a questioning look, and he nodded.

"Yes, she is correct. I am not very hungry yet either."

"All right then," Luke replied with a grin. "Off to the ranch we go. I know Dylan is looking forward to meeting the two of you."

THEY REACHED the ranch twenty minutes later. Isabella was impressed. She'd seen ranches in passing, but she'd never gone to one directly or seen one up close.

There was quite a lot of action going on when she got there. A man was standing on the second step from the ground, his arms raised as well as his voice as he called out directions. Men were walking all around the front of the compound, carrying various heavy items, stacks of shingles, lumber, buckets of items Isabella couldn't see.

The sound of dogs barking frantically got Isabella's attention. She focused on a group of men gathered together in a staggered circle. When they parted enough for her to see, she was delighted when she saw three dogs in the middle of the circle, playing with each other. Isabella was willing to bet they were siblings, and it was clear they were playing happily. There was no growling, no biting, no bared teeth.

The dogs did kick up on their back legs and paw at each other with the front two, but it was a mild form of friendly boxing, and the men were all laughing and cheering them on. Some of them were imitating the dogs, rolling their eyes, and kicking out a back leg like they'd seen the ladies do.

Isabella let her eyes roam over the scenery. So many men, some working, some playing, most of them looked happy. Even some of the ones who were digging holes to plant the trees another ranch hand was holding as they stood nearby. She heard one of the men holding a tree, teasing the hole digger, saying he wasn't going fast enough and the tree would plan roots right where he was standing if the job wasn't done soon. The other man just chucked his chin up in the air once and continued doing his task.

As they rolled up to the front porch of the massive main house, Isabella caught sight of a large orange cat sitting on the edge of the porch. The animal's tail was switching back and forth. Isabella felt a sudden, very strong urge to go and pet the cat.

As soon as the buggy came to a stop, she got down and hurried up the steps to the top, going at an angle, so she was approaching the cat directly. She wanted to be in front of its sight so that it would see her coming. The last thing she wanted to do was scare the thing.

It didn't look in the least bit frightened. It was

such a big cat, she imagined it dominated its personal animal world. She stopped a foot or so away, staying still before bending at the waist and bringing her face close to the cat's. She reached out slowly to brush her fingers on the cat's front paw.

The animal looked at her through narrow eyes. Now the very end of the tail was the only thing twitching.

She blinked at the animal and stayed silent for a moment. She was trying to show that she wasn't aggressive toward it. It didn't even move a muscle other than its tail. Isabella felt confident enough to get closer and pet it on its head. It closed its eyes and began to purr.

"Awww, look at you," she said in the smoothest voice she could muster. "How handsome you are." She'd decided he was a boy. Female cats could get that large, but usually, they weren't. She looked up at Luke. "Do you know its name?"

He gave her a look before saying, "Of course. His name is Gus."

Once again, Isabella felt surprised. "Gus," she repeated. She noticed when she said his name, the animal's eyes opened slightly wider. He was staring at her like she was another cat. She giggled. "I like that name. You look like a Gus, yes, you do. *Si, il mio prezioso gatto.*"

She heard Lo behind her mumbling to Luke, "She said he's a precious cat."

She chided herself silently. She needed to remember to only speak English. There weren't going to be many people fluent in Italian in Bighorn, Texas, and Lo wouldn't always be with her to explain what she was saying.

She stood up straight, petting the cat once more, and gave Luke a big smile. "I love kitty-cats," she said, forcing any Italian accent from her voice. "I already like this ranch and Bighorn itself. I'm so glad I came."

The look of delight and appreciation on Luke's face filled Isabella's heart with joy.

"Come on," he said, waving one hand and holding the door open for them this time. "Let's go see where Dylan is. I'm willing to bet he's in his office. He spends most of his time there if he's not out in the field. He knows we're coming, so he won't be out there. Unless there's an emergency."

Isabella noticed the drop in his volume with the last sentence. She followed him with Lo by her side, gazing all around her. Luke seemed to forget they hadn't been in the huge house before. He stormed through the large foyer like he had a real purpose. Isabella wanted to tell him to wait a minute so she could look around at all the beautiful decorations, artwork, sculptured pieces that were placed in strategic areas to make it look more aesthetically pleasing.

She was impressed with what she did get to see. The stairs going to the second-floor landing were in the middle of the foyer. There were two hallways on either side, leading to the back and sides of the house.

"His office is down here," Luke threw over his shoulder before stopping so abruptly Isabella almost ran into him. She halted in place and gripped Lo's hand tighter to get him to stop, as well.

He pulled his hand away just when Luke turned to them, a sheepish look on his face.

"I am so sorry. This isn't my house, so I've been a terrible host. There's the stairs, as you can see. The parlor and the den are on that side of the house. There is a storage room at the back of the house. On this side, we have the kitchen and dining room. There is an additional storage cellar for cold things below the house and also a second kitchen where I think slaves used to be. I don't think it's been used in a long time. Dylan bought this place as it was, and it had been vacant for long enough that he had—or is having to do—extensive repairs."

"I'm sure he loves the work, though, doesn't he?"

Luke tilted his head to the side, his expression impressed. "Yeah," he replied. "He does."

14

———

Three days later, Isabella and Lo had already settled into their jobs. She was thrilled to have her own desk and had placed the only picture she owned—that of her mother and father a few days before the siblings left Italy for America—prominently on her desk. She proudly told anyone who even glanced at the picture who was in it. If they had time, she told them a story or two of her village and the people in it.

By that third day, Isabella was sure she had made friends with at least half the people in town. That was sure to be an exaggeration, but that was how she felt. It wasn't just customers who visited the press office. It was all of Dylan's friends and Luke's friends and Dylan's wife, Mattie's friends. They all wanted to meet her. She didn't know what Luke and Dylan told them about her, but they were all smiling when they came in, and she didn't get any bad feelings from any of them.

The ladies came bearing sweets and meals in containers they said she could return later "at her leisure". The men gave her advice and told her what parts of town and specifically who to steer clear of if she didn't want drama in her life.

Isabella was delighted that they all treated her with respect. That was very important to her. When she gave someone respect, she desired the same in return. When she didn't get it, her opinion of the person would not be a good one.

So Isabella and Lo were happy with their lot in life so far, enjoying the adventure their father had sent them on.

The house Luke had given them to stay in was huge, as far as she was concerned. Their own family home in Italy was large, but it wasn't as big as Luke's. Dylan's farm was three times the size of their home in Italy. And had much, much more land connected to it, as well.

Isabella decided on that third day as she returned from the press that she wanted to do some exploring. Luke had told them the house was theirs until they found a place of their own. He hadn't given them any restrictions on where they could go. She'd found a room with a lot of books in it, several desks and tables with fancy lamps and lanterns set on them. She assumed it was a makeshift library. It was very unkempt, which led her to think it was probably a room of Dylan's. Luke had said he wasn't the cleanliest of sorts.

It was the first room she went to after she'd cleaned up and changed into something more relaxing. She didn't feel the need to be dressed fine while inside the house. She had no one to impress. Lo had seen her with her hair a mess and a face swollen from sickness. He wasn't likely to mention her casualness.

She pushed open the door and poked her head in. There was plenty of light in the room as the sun beamed in bright through all the windows. That was one thing she noticed about the entire house. Each room had at least one window. Most of them had two. Others had three, and some even four. The architect who had designed it must have been anxious to have plenty of sunlight. Or just really liked windows.

Isabella was impressed. She smiled, going into the room and closing the door behind her, leaving it cracked an inch or so. The first thing she did was go to the tall shelves against the wall. There were many fascinating titles. She ran her finger over them, tilting her head to the side so she could read the words on the spine.

Journey to the Center of the Earth... Moby Dick... Alice and the Looking Glass... Moby Dick... Around the World in Eighty Days...

Isabella was taken aback to see these books that her father had worked so hard to find. He sought the best copies to give to her for holidays. They were all lined up right here... *with dust on their covers...*

How could Luke and Dylan have let these books get in such a condition? She was offended by their lack of care.

Isabella felt the sudden strong urge to clean. She looked around for something she could use to dust off the books and the shelves they were stacked on. In the desk nearby, sticking out of one of the drawers, was a piece of cloth. She went straight for it and pulled the drawer open to pull the rest of it out.

Removing the cloth revealed a leather-bound book that immediately caught Isabella's eye. She had to know what it was. Clutching the dusting cloth in one hand, she withdrew the journal from the drawer and leaned back against the desk, looking down at it.

She ran one finger over the soft leather. It had no title. The pages inside were a dull white color. They didn't look like regular paper. They were soft, like the leather cover. She wondered what type of material it was.

Isabella pulled the strap from the buckle and opened the book to the middle.

She saw handwriting and knew it must be a journal. She wondered how old it must be, considering the state of the "library" itself. This journal could be a hundred years old.

She ran her eyes over the handwriting first, analyzing it in her mind. It was somewhat blockish, easy to read, and didn't have too much of a flourish. Then, at the bottom of the page, the signature was large and had all the flourish the regular handwriting did not have.

She was impressed by the signature, even though she couldn't read the name.

Isabella lifted her eyes to the entry, which said May 4. There was no year, which she thought was odd. Perhaps it was one year per journal?

She shook her head to clear her thoughts and read a passage from the book.

Aside from the fact that I have recently married, there have been other changes that have caused him to show some signs of deep despair and loneliness. There doesn't appear to be anything I can do about it, as I am, in fact, not a woman who can give him the comfort he needs. I am his best friend, and I am deeply worried about him. Perhaps this new venture will bring him the happiness my friend so richly deserves. It is my hope.

Isabella hung on the last four words. She frowned. Dylan had married but not recently. This was Dylan's journal, she was sure of it.

Ashamed that she had read such intimate words about who she could only assume was Luke, she replaced the journal and left the room, her heart heavy for her new boss.

15

I sabella heard the men's voices in Luke's office from her desk. His door was cracked open about six inches.

Their discussion was obviously not confidential. They were talking in very casual tones. Isabella could tell what good friends they were by the way they spoke to each other. If she hadn't known otherwise, she would have thought they were brothers.

"What's that you got there?" Dylan asked. "You look really interested in it."

"It's a letter," Luke responded. "A reply to the ad I put in the magazine."

Isabella's skin tingled. Luke had used his own magazine to advertise for a bride? Why would he need to do that? He was handsome, intelligent, made money, was obviously a good-hearted individual. The list of his good traits went on and on. He shouldn't need to advertise for a wife. Isabella couldn't help listening, though she pretended she was engrossed in the book she had open in front of her on the desk.

"How many have you gotten so far?" Dylan continued.

"Three. These two..." Isabella heard the scoffing in his voice, "I don't know why they want to be mail order brides, but they didn't appeal to me at all. This one here... maybe. I'll have to take it home and read it again. Give it a think. I'm not in a hurry. I'd really like to wait for a letter that really catches my attention, y' see?"

"What exactly are you looking for?"

There was a pause, and Isabella crammed that moment with thoughts of her own version of perfect for Luke. The thing was—she had all of those qualities she was thinking about. She pressed her lips together, feeling her cheeks growing hot. Could she allow feelings to grow in her heart for her boss? She had just arrived and was still getting used to being in Texas. The townsfolk were quite friendly to her and Lo. She felt more and more at home every day.

Would she be shunned and vilified if she let

herself have feelings for Luke since he was her boss and had brought her and Lo from New York on his own dime, just like one of the mail order brides in his magazine? She didn't want the townsfolk to turn on her.

"I'm looking for a woman who has a brain but won't try to override me at every turn. Someone creative, a woman who wants to laugh and smile more than frown and cry."

"I think most men want a woman like that," Dylan added. "At least the last part. I know plenty of men who don't want a woman to be smart. Not their woman, anyway."

"That's a sign of insecurity," Luke responded. "I'm not insecure. I want to have intelligent conversations with my wife, not order her around and follow up behind her to make sure she's done what she's supposed to do. We left that kind of mindset behind already. I don't know why I ever thought that way."

"You didn't, really," Dylan responded. "I was more the one who thought women should be seen and not heard. Like children. That's what I thought growing up."

Isabella was surprised to hear those words. She would never have expected Luke or Dylan to be chauvinists. Then again, she'd only known either of them for about a week.

"You don't think like that now, and neither do I," Luke confirmed.

"What's the main thing you're looking for in your woman?" Dylan asked. "You'd think that would be something I'd know but doggone if I can't remember ever really knowing if you had a type of woman or not."

Again, there was a pause. Isabella waited anxiously to hear what Luke had to say next.

"I reckon I don't really have a type. I just want a good woman. Good heart. Good brain. Good personality. I want a woman who will be nice to our children and won't be pushy and angry and resentful and jealous."

"You might have a problem with that last one," Dylan replied, laughter underlying his words.

"You're probably right," Luke said in a serious voice. "I won't have women falling all over me until I have a woman on my arm."

Both men laughed. She heard them shuffling around and tried to keep her cheeks from flushing because she'd been eavesdropping. Luke's door swung open, and the two men emerged.

"I'm hoping you find the right woman, Luke. You

want any advice, you know where to find me."

Luke laughed. "I sure do." He walked with Dylan to the front door.

"Let's go to lunch," Dylan suggested abruptly, holding up one hand as if he had just had the best idea in the world, and he didn't know why he hadn't thought of it before.

Luke pulled a watch from his pocket and flipped open the lid so he could see what time it was. "It is nearing twelve. Yeah, let's go get something to eat."

When he looked at Isabella, she was sure she looked like the cat that ate the canary. But she smiled and tried to relax her features so he wouldn't notice.

"Izzie, we really don't need to keep the office open for lunch. Anyone who needs to place something in our magazine has plenty of time before the next issue. Why don't you grab something to eat? I'm sure your brother wouldn't mind if you brought him a nice lunch at the ranch."

Isabella's mind ran all over the place. At first, she'd thought he was going to ask if she wanted to go to lunch with them. Then, when it became obvious that wasn't what he was asking her, she wondered if he suggested getting food for Lo because he wanted to get her to Dylan's ranch.

She chided herself for being silly. What would he want to get her to Dylan's ranch for? Just because he was staying there temporarily until she and Lo found their own place? She'd been stunned when she found out Luke had left his home so they could occupy it without feeling uncomfortable—any more than they already did staying in someone else's home.

"I... I'll do that. Thank you for the suggestion, Luke."

He grinned and nodded before the two men stepped through the doorway. Dylan waved to her, and she waved back, giggling softly.

Once the door was closed and the men were gone, Isabella immediately went into Luke's office. She couldn't help feeling envious of the women writing to Luke. How could she stand a chance when they were now throwing themselves at her?

Normally, Isabella would have felt like a scoundrel going through someone else's mail. But all she wanted was to find out what address Luke had used for his letters and if there was a code she needed to use for the address. The code was placed in all the magazines as part of the return address so that the recipient would know which issue the sender got their address from.

Luke had placed his ad in the first magazine they printed. She didn't know if it had a code or not.

It didn't take her long to find the envelope addressed to Luke from one of the women. The only reason Isabella spotted the three envelopes was that the one on the very top had big swooping handwriting and a woman's name in the return area.

She was nervous but only took a glance at the envelope, making a mental note of the address Luke used. Then she turned and scanned the room for a copy of the very first magazine. She was sure Luke kept a copy of it in there, even though only one other had come out since the first. She saw not one but two copies of the magazine sitting on a table just below the window.

Isabella hurried to pick one up and flip through it. She found what she was looking for on the last page, halfway down. Luke Turner. That was his name. She read his "requirements" and wished she had seen the ad when she first picked up the magazine.

Her eyes lifted, and she found herself looking through the glass into the eyes of her smiling brother. Laughing, she folded the magazine on her finger, grabbed her skirt with her other hand, and hurried to the front door to let him in.

16

J ust as Lo was coming into the office, Penelope came out of the press room. She had her hat and gloves on. It appeared she was done for the day, and she was in quite a hurry to leave. She skittered across the floor, reminding Isabella even more of a mouse. Her smile was cast first to Isabella and then Lo.

"I must go, my dear," she said. "I have told Luke I will be taking off early today. I have family matters to attend to."

"Oh, well, I hope everything is all right," Isabella said, stepping back. "I will pray for your family."

Penelope's smile drew out her lips further. "Oh, it is not a serious matter. Just a necessary task that must be performed. You take care, both of you. I will see you tomorrow."

Isabella would gladly have given the woman a goodbye, but she was out the door and down the street before either of them could react. They did share an amazed look that the woman could move so fast.

"Well, she seems nice. From the few seconds I saw her." Lo grinned at his sister.

"Yes, she really is. But she is so…" Isabella let her words drift off, trying to think of the perfect way to describe the little woman that had just left. "Energetic, I suppose is the word," she concluded. "Yes, that must be what it is. She's energetic and reminds me of a little critter just racing back and forth all the time."

"She does not have a very energetic job," Lo remarked, his eyes drifting to the backroom Penelope had just left.

"That is true. Maybe that is why she spends her energy when she is doing everything else." Isabella grabbed her brother's arm, surprising him and making him widen his eyes at her. "I have to tell you what I have discovered and what I have been doing, Lo. I hope you don't think badly of me because of it."

"Uh-oh. What have you been doing, *sorella*?"

"I have discovered that Luke is a very lonely man," Isabella began, pulling Lo to the chair in front of her desk. "Let me gather my things, and we will go out for some food to eat. I want to tell you what I have decided."

"I am anxious to hear," Lo said in a voice that was genuine.

Isabella grabbed her bag and her jacket and gloves, hurrying to the door, which Lo held open for her. She passed him by with a smile and a thank you.

Once they were outside, she held up her notebook and pen, so it was in his line of vision. "I'm going to write a letter," she said eagerly.

"Is that so?" Lo asked, raising his eyebrows as if that was the most surprising thing she could possibly have told him. "And who are you writing to? Mother and Father? Please send them my love."

Isabella shook her head, giving him a secretive smile. "No, this letter isn't to Mother and Father." She looked around to see if anyone was listening in to her conversation. No one was paying attention to her other than men across the street taking a second glance her way like they always did. They weren't close enough to hear what she was saying, though. Still, she stepped a little closer to her brother and murmured loudly, "I'm going to write to Luke."

Lo's eyebrows shot up again, and he blinked at her.

"Why are you writing to him when he is right here to speak to."

Isabella glanced around nervously. "Where?"

Lo pursed his lips and narrowed his eyes, looking at her under hooded lids. "Izzie. Not right *here* here. He's here somewhere. You don't have to write to him. Explain yourself. You are teasing me."

Isabella laughed softly, jostling her brother with her elbow. "I do not mean to, *mio fratello*. I am writing to him because I have decided that I am the perfect woman to fill the spot he desires to fill."

"I didn't know he was looking for a bride."

"Yes, apparently, he does not find a woman here that is attractive to him in all ways. But he said something to Dylan about the woman he is looking for, and I think I will do nicely. I know how to have a conversation. I am well-versed in English literature, so we could discuss books if he wishes. When I do not know something, I do not hesitate to ask. I love to learn. I am sure he will find that attractive about me."

Lo took a step away from her and gave her a scan from head to toe and back. "You have much to offer a man, Izzie. Make sure he is the man you want, too. Do you find him attractive? Do you believe you would be happy with him should he ask you to marry him?"

Isabella hadn't thought about the future quite so vividly as she did when her brother asked her those questions. She imagined Luke asking her to marry him and let the warm feeling wash over her body. She closed her eyes, reveling in the feeling before it flittered away on the wings of a dream.

"I do think I would be happy with him," she said breathlessly. "He is so handsome and smart. He is a kind man, as well, and generous. What can I find that is a fault of his? I cannot find even one when I think about it carefully."

Lo smiled at her. "Then I am anxious to know your plan so that I can help you. What are you going to do?"

Isabella felt a strong surge of affection for her brother. She grabbed him in a surprise hug that made him let out all his breath in an "oof" before she let him go. She kept hold of his arms, though, and couldn't help bouncing on the balls of her feet. She clapped her hands lightly. "Come on. We will go to the restaurant, and I will write a letter to him. You can help me with it. And then I will go to the postmaster and ask them to give it to Luke."

"But they will tell him it is you that sent him the letter," Lo reasoned.

Isabella thought about it for a moment, touching her chin with one finger and looking up. "I shall just have to ask them not to tell him. I believe if I am nice enough, they will do me this favor. Do you agree?"

Lo smiled wide, nodding at her. His positive nature made her feel all the more confident that her plan would work.

"Yes, *si*, that is a good idea. Let us go for food and write this letter."

"I must stop at the mercantile and get some paper and an envelope."

"Do you have a pen?"

Isabella laughed delightedly. She was excited about what they were going to do and hopeful that her plan would work. She didn't want to be petty. But those other ladies wouldn't be good enough for Luke. She could feel it in her bones.

Laughing at her silly thoughts, Isabella pulled a pen from her purse and held it up in the air, waving it back and forth.

"It's the only thing I already have," she exclaimed.

They both laughed as they hurried across the street to the mercantile.

17

Luke didn't return to the press office that day. He spent the rest of the day going around town talking to investors in the magazine, ending it with a conference between himself, Dylan, and Judge Carter, who was the biggest investor of all.

When he found himself in front of the house he had occupied with Dylan for years before Dylan bought the ranch, he realized how tired he was. He wasn't staying there. He had to go all the way through town to the other side and go out to the Sullivan ranch if he wanted to go "home".

And Luke definitely wanted to go home. It was time for some rest and relaxation.

He turned his horse away from the house and headed back through town down the main road.

He saw when Harry, the messenger boy who worked for the postmaster, came running out of the office, his eyes directly on Luke. He slowed his horse and then brought it to a stop when the boy was not far away. He leaned all the way down, holding his hand out.

Harry lifted the envelope in the air to give it to him. "Don't know how this missed ya this mornin', Mr. Turner, I'm sorry. It looks like it's from New York."

It was the first time Harry had ever pointed out where a letter was from. Luke had been under the impression the boy never looked. He took the letter, leaving his eyes on the boy.

"Is that so?"

"Yeah, that's what it says on the envelope," Harry continued, much to Luke's surprise. He'd never had a real conversation with the boy before. He was amused by it and gave Harry a smile.

"So it does." He glanced at the envelope to show he was invested in the conversation. "That's a long way from here, isn't it?"

"Yeah, it is." For some reason, Harry looked very satisfied with himself. His grin was stretched from ear to ear, and his eyes twinkled brightly. "Well, you enjoy your letter from New York, Mr. Turner. Bye." He saluted quickly and took off back toward the post office. He didn't go in, though. Luke watched him jump up on the wooden walkway and take off in the direction he himself was going.

Luke urged his horse to move again and looked down at the envelope as he rode to Dylan's ranch. He opened it along the way and read the words written there.

The first thing he noticed was that the handwriting was somewhat familiar. For some reason, though, it seemed more masculine than feminine handwriting. Like it was written by a man. The words, however, sounded more feminine. He dismissed his initial impression and read it through, enjoying it immensely. It felt like God above had heard what he'd been telling Dylan that morning.

This woman was an avid reader. She enjoyed books of all kinds and enjoyed talking about them. She longed for adventure and fun and didn't wish to be a meek wallflower, only living to serve another. She sounded energetic and upbeat.

He dropped his eyes to the name written at the bottom. With large, swooping letters, he read the name *Dolly Bean*. His heart thumped harder for a moment. He stared at the sweet name, taken in by the way it sounded. It was more a term of endearment than a formal name, surely.

He smiled. This was the letter he'd been waiting for. And to think he'd just been mentioning these very things to Dylan that morning. He looked up at the sky, grinning. He knew who he had to thank for this blessing.

Luke whistled a happy tune the rest of the way to Dylan's ranch. He was anxious to tell his best friend all about Dolly, the apparent woman of his dreams.

He found Dylan sitting on the porch, enjoying the sunset. It was the perfect moment to tell him about the letter. His wife, Mattie, was sitting beside him on the long porch swing. Dylan had his arms stretched across the back of the swing, behind her on one side.

They both smiled at Luke as he hopped up the steps to the porch. He held up the letter triumphantly, his eyes on his friend.

"Luke!" Dylan said his name like he hadn't seen him in years. "How was your day?"

"It hasn't ended yet," Luke replied vehemently, grinning. "You'll never guess what I got here."

"It looks like a letter." It was Mattie who spoke.

Luke was surprised by how excited she looked when her eyes rested on the envelope.

"It's a letter from a woman," Luke confirmed, nodding, "in response to my ad in the magazine. It isn't just any letter, though." He laughed, unable to believe his luck. "It's a letter from the perfect woman. Remember what I was telling you this morning? You asked me what I was looking for? What type of woman I really want? I'm tellin' you, fella, that woman is in this letter. Harry delivered it to me as I was leaving town. Said he didn't know why it wasn't delivered this mornin' with the others."

"Well, don't just stand there. Let me read it." Dylan lifted his arm from behind Mattie and held out his hand to take the envelope.

He proceeded to remove the letter, unfold it, and quickly read it. He tilted it slightly toward his wife, and she leaned in so she could read it at the same time. Her smile grew wider as she read it. Luke was a little taken aback, however, by Dylan's reaction. He looked amused.

"You got this letter this afternoon?" he asked, sliding his eyes to Luke, who nodded.

"Yeah, that's right. Why do you look like that? What are you thinking?"

"It's really fitting," he said, folding the letter and

sliding it back in the envelope. "I suggest you write to her right away."

Luke took the letter but turned suspicious eyes to his friend. "You had a strange look on your face there for a minute, Dylan. Care to tell me what you were thinking?"

"It's just really close to what you were saying this morning, don't you think?"

"Yeah, I do. I think the big man above is lookin' out for me. He heard my prayer."

Marie's eyes widened. "You were praying this morning in your office?"

"No," Luke responded, looking at her. "But I have been praying for this woman for a while now. And I think He heard me."

"Well, I'm happy for you," Marie said definitively. She looked sharply at her husband. "And Dylan is happy for you, too. He's just nervous that you're going to be hurt."

"I didn't say that," Dylan huffed, giving his wife a pouty look. She laughed and swatted at him playfully.

"It doesn't make you look bad to care about if your friend's feelings get hurt, Dylan."

He shifted in the seat, letting his eyes roam back

to Luke, who was enjoying the scene between them immensely.

"That's not the point."

"It is, and you know it," Mattie teased him.

Dylan looked directly at Luke, narrowing his eyes and sharpening his tone. "You just be careful with that, Luke. She's right that I don't want to see you gettin' hurt by some random woman who only wants to take advantage of you. I just want you to be happy. Nothin' wrong with that. My best friend and all." He was grumbling by the time he was done, looking at Mattie instead of Luke.

Luke chuckled, tapping his friend on the leg with the envelope. "Thanks for caring, Dylan. I'll be careful, I promise. I won't let her hurt my feelings."

He and Mattie laughed while Dylan just grinned, looking away from them.

18

E ach day that passed gave Luke another reason to appreciate hiring Isabella to run the front office. She was so friendly and personable. Every time someone came in, they went straight to her and just started talking. She was intelligent and didn't have to continually ask him or Dylan questions. He'd heard her consult with Penelope a few times, but it was usually about the spelling of an English word. She wanted to know if she got it right.

As far as he knew, she always did.

He was on his way to Dylan's ranch for a dinner party. He knew all the people that would be there, but for some reason, he was anxious to see what

Isabella was doing. She was good for conversation when he was bored. And other times, too.

He let his horse meander down the path, looking ahead to the lot in front of the ranch. It was filled with buggies and horses tied to the makeshift hitching rails Dylan's men had put in, so everyone had a place to leave their transportation.

The Bendalls, the Morcrofts, the Windinghams... he saw the couples in his head when he saw their buggies. It was the same with the horses. He saw the riders in his head, recognizing either the animal or the saddle.

It seemed like he was the last guest.

As soon as he thought that, Luke saw another horse coming down the path. He'd turned to the left to find an empty slot at the hitching rail and caught sight of her out of the corner of his eye. He felt a tension in his chest but ignored it, smiling at her.

"Mare Lawson," he said, tipping his hat to her. He could tell by the look on her face that she was delighted to see him. She was one of the few women in town who'd shown interest in him. Unfortunately, much as he would have liked it, he couldn't bring himself to feel anything more than friendship for her. She was lovely to look at, her blond hair piled high on her head with still more draping down over her shoulders, snapping blue eyes, and a pouty mouth that gave the impression no crosswords would ever cross it.

"Well, look at you, Luke. Don't you look handsome. Are you dressing up for a certain young lady?"

Was that suspicion and jealousy he saw behind the blue in her eyes?

He chuckled. "Nothing like that," he said, sliding out of his saddle and waiting for her to take a space near him. She was soon standing next to him, giving him that longing look she always had in her eyes. "I'm here on my own for now."

She raised her eyebrows, hooking her hand around his elbow. Her gesture made him once again wish he could bring his heart to feel the love for her that she so desired. "For now? Do we have prospects?"

He responded with a mysterious expression. "We will see."

"Hmmm," she murmured. They walked together to the porch and up the steps.

When they got to the door, he held his hand out for her to proceed in front of him. "I'm going around to the side entrance, Mare. I'll see you inside."

Luke crossed to the left side of the wrap-around deck and hurried to a side door that would take him into the kitchen. He didn't want to leave her enough time to say she would come with him. She was a step in the doorway when he'd bolted anyway, so he didn't expect her to follow behind him.

He stepped into the side door, closing it behind him and leaning against it, looking at the cook and two helpers who had been hired for the evening. They had stopped what they were doing and were now staring at him with amused eyes.

He grinned, showing his teeth together and slipped past them.

"Sorry about that. I, uh, I…"

"Trying to escape a lusty lady?" the cook, a short, round woman, said with a pleasant grin.

He felt his cheeks grow hot and nodded but couldn't find the words. He left the kitchen in a hurry and went looking for Dylan.

The dining room was almost full when he went in. Most of the guests were already seated. Small place cards had been set in front of the plates, but Luke already knew where he was sitting. It was the same place he always sat.

He was pleasantly surprised to see Isabella and Lo had been seated next to him, with Isabella at his right and Lo in the seat after her. She was already there, chatting with the woman across from her.

Luke's heart thumped harder when he sat down and saw the joy on her face when she looked at him.

"Good evening," she said enthusiastically. "It is a lovely evening, isn't it?"

"Yes," Luke replied with a firm nod. "The weather was warm today."

"I was able to secure three new accounts for the magazine today," Isabella stated, her smile growing. "And their advertisements will bring in—"

"No shop talk tonight," Luke said, lifting a finger and placing it on her lips. Her eyes widened, and he immediately removed it, worried that he'd over-stepped. "I'm sorry. I didn't mean to... I think we should concentrate on having a good time tonight and not worry about the magazine. What do you say?"

He could tell she was pleased with that idea. She nodded.

"*Si.* Yes. Lovely."

LUKE SPENT most of that night tagging along behind Isabella wherever she went. He didn't mean to be a pest, which he told her when he found her in

Dylan's library, looking at the newest collection of books his friend had purchased.

"These books," she said, turning back to them after sufficiently reproaching him for giving her a start when he came in. She swept her hand in front of the shelf. "They are classic books, most of them. Some of them are brand new."

"Yes, that's right. You have a good eye for literature."

She pulled her eyebrows together, looking up at him. "But there in the house that you have kindly let us stay in... there is a room of books there, as well. And they are covered in dust and dirt. They have not been opened or read for many years. It is a shame to let them dissolve to dust in that manner."

"Do you want to pull 'em out and dust 'em off?" Luke asked, giving her a questioning look. "I'm sure Dylan won't mind. And if they belong to me, then yeah, go right ahead. Honestly, I don't know what's in some of the rooms at that house. We just put things in different places, you know, to get them out of the way."

"It looked to be an office of some kind."

"Oh, probably Dylan's office."

"I apologize if I was not supposed to enter that room."

Luke chuckled, shaking his head. "No, really, you can go anywhere. I don't have any secrets to hide, and I'm thinking Dylan doesn't either. I can't be a hundred percent on that, but I can be pretty sure. Maybe 99%. Or 95%." He winked at her. "You never know some people."

She giggled, covering her mouth with one hand. He liked that sound. She was a good woman to be friends with. Maybe she could give him some advice on how to best attract a woman. That way, when Dolly got to town, if he invited her, he would know what to do to make her feel special and cared for.

But was that something he wanted to ask Isabella?

It was certainly something to think about anyway.

19

___

Luke stepped out of the post office after leaving his letter for Dolly with them. He was settling in for a two-week-or-so wait before he would get one back from her.

He clapped his hands together and rubbed them in a satisfying way, casting his gaze down the street outside. There was plenty of action for a Friday afternoon. The weekend always proved to be packed with activities in Bighorn.

After his evening with Isabella at Dylan's dinner party, Luke felt ready and willing to give the right woman a chance. So far, of the five letters he'd received, he liked Dolly's the most. It had a familiar ring to it, which made him feel like they would have a deeper connection.

He stopped abruptly when he saw Dylan and Lo coming out of the lumber yard office. Crossing the street on nimble feet, he jogged over to them, lifting one hand in a wave. "Howdy," he called out. "What are ya doin' in town?"

"Gettin' some supplies for that new shed we're buildin' on the property."

Luke shook hands with them both, giving Lo a big grin. "I see our new friend is coming along nicely."

"Oh, yeah," Dylan said, turning his gaze to the young man. "He's a fast learner and a hard worker. But let us not stand here and talk about him like he's not even standing right here with us." Dylan tilted his head back and let out a sharp laugh. "What are you doing out here instead of sitting behind that desk of yours getting some work done?"

"I decided to mail a letter, thank you," Luke huffed. He knew the look on his face would give away his joke. "Can't just live for work, you know."

"That is true. So which of the ladies did you write to this time?"

Luke noticed the highly curious look on Lo's face. The young man looked like he was hanging on every word, waiting for the answer Luke was about to give with bated breath.

"I told you about Dolly, didn't I?" he asked, directing the question to Dylan, even though Lo was the one who obviously really wanted to know. Maybe he was planning on placing an ad himself. Luke didn't really think he would need to. He was handsome, young, and available. He could probably get any woman he wanted. Mare came to Luke's mind, but he pushed the thought away. He was not a matchmaker.

"She's the one I just sent a letter to. She's... interesting."

"Did you write to many women?" Lo asked curiously.

Luke shook his head. "I received a handful of letters, but Dolly's was the only one I really found interest in. I did write a letter to another lady, but I never sent it." He looked at Dylan. "Remember when you asked me about that?"

"Yeah," Dylan replied, nodding. He tilted his head to look around Luke's, prompting Luke to turn around to see what his friend was looking at. Several young men, including the boy Harry, who was usually a messenger, were loading planks of wood into the back of Dylan's wagon.

"If you want any advice on those matters," Lo put in, getting their attention back, "you should speak to

Izzie. She is very knowledgeable in matters of the heart."

"Is that so?" Luke asked, a pleasant feeling filling his chest.

In a short time, Isabella had proved herself to be invaluable.

Lo nodded vigorously. "Oh yes. In Italy, she was well-known for giving good advice on relationships. She does not think just with the head but also with the heart. And she is not one-sided when a couple is having an argument."

Luke chuckled. "Thank you for that, Lo. When I need advice, I certainly know where to go. Fortunately, there are no arguments for our dear Izzie to solve, is there?"

"Yes, we do not want that," Lo agreed, laughing softly. "You cannot have arguments when you do not even know the lady."

"Well, I'll talk to her if I need anything," Luke said, "and I appreciate the suggestion."

"Where is Isabella anyway?" Dylan asked. "We passed the office and didn't see her inside."

Luke shook his head. "I have no idea where she is right now. I haven't been in the office since early this morning, and she was already hard at work with Penelope in the back. She's training, you know. She wants to know everything about the press and how it works. Pretty soon, she'll be able to run the whole show all by herself. We won't even be needed anymore."

Dylan laughed. "I'm already not needed, Luke. You take care of everything now that I'm at the ranch. And I'm thankful for it. I'll just sit back and continue to be the silent partner."

"You weren't silent at the beginning," Luke quipped and laughed when Dylan gave him a droll look. "Oh, I'm not complaining about the new you, Dylan. Don't worry about that."

Dylan laughed with him.

"Well, they've got the wood loaded up, Luke. We'll talk later, eh? You come by tomorrow after-noon, and we'll talk shop for a while. Maybe come up with some new concepts for the magazine so we can add to it. More stories and anecdotes. Maybe add a cartoon if we can find an artist here in Bighorn."

"That's a project for Izzie," Luke stated firmly. He could just see the beautiful Italian woman asking everyone she met if they could draw a cartoon. She was friendly enough. She would find someone, he had no doubt of that.

"I will mention it to her when I see her if you like," Lo suggested.

Luke grinned at him. "Better not just yet," he said. "Dylan and I will discuss it later on."

"All right, I'm gonna head on to the house then," Lo said enthusiastically, looking at both men one after the other. Luke smiled at him, nodding.

"You need anything while I'm here?" Dylan asked.

Luke was a bit surprised by his friend's question. It wasn't that Dylan was a stingy man. He was generous, to be sure. But for him to offer to buy a stranger —an employee—*anything* they needed was a first. Luke's heart warmed over just a little bit as a strong surge of appreciation for his friend filled him.

"No, sir, but thank you for asking," Lo responded. "I do suppose Izzie would be the one to ask, but she is not here. I am sure we will be fine. Thank you again."

He backed away from them, his face alight with excitement. Luke wondered what was making the young man so exhilarated.

Must be nice to be so excited about nothing, he thought, amused by the young man. He reminded Luke of Harry, in a way, though Harry was much younger. It wasn't immaturity that reminded Luke of

Harry. It was innocence. Luke very much liked the innocence of Lorenzo and his sister.

When Lo had backed away about five feet, he spun around on one heel and took off down the wooden walkway.

"He's not going to help you unload this wood when you get back?" Luke asked, watching the boy leave.

"No, he's not really strong enough for that and… I'm thinking he might be better put to use inside the house, but I already have a butler. So I'm giving him the stables so he can take care of the horses. He's really good at that."

"They're nice young people, aren't they?" Luke mused softly.

Dylan responded with a gentle nod and a voice that was just as smooth. "Yes, they are."

20

Isabella was downstairs when she heard Lo come bursting through the door upstairs, calling her name. He was stomping through the house, and she couldn't help hurrying to the bottom of the stairs and calling up to him.

"Lo. I'm down here in the cellar getting meat for our dinners. Come down here and talk to me." She turned and went back to the waist-high table where she was sorting through different types of meat. He had ceased his stomping, so she had to assume he'd heard her. A few moments later, she heard his boots thumping down the stairs and could see first his legs, then his torso, then his head as he leaned down to look at her.

"There you are. I thought you'd disappeared.

And right now. That would be very bad timing, I must say."

"What are you talking about, Lo?" Isabella asked, eyeing her brother with amusement. She picked up a long slab of meat and began to untie the strings to unwrap the brown paper. She didn't know what it was as it wasn't labeled. Nothing in the cold cellar had been labeled. She was left wondering how Luke and Dylan ever knew what they were having for dinner. Maybe they didn't. Maybe they had waited until they unwrapped the paper and gave themselves a surprise every night.

Isabella giggled, squinting to focus on the knot that was battling against her and winning so far.

"I'm talking about your letter. You are Dolly, are you not? Is that not what name you gave yourself?"

"Oh yes." Isabella was struck with a jolt of adrenaline. She immediately forgot about the wrapped meat and stared at her brother with wide eyes. "What have you heard? Has Luke said something? Has he mentioned Dolly to you?"

"He wrote to you today." Lo spoke in a tremendously triumphant voice, his face shining with pride and satisfaction. He was standing straight with his shoulders squared. Isabella could tell he was happy he had been the one to tell her the good news. She was glad he was on board with her plan. If he had fought against her, she most likely would not have gone through with it.

She pressed her small hands against her chest. "Me? He wrote to me?"

"As Dolly, of course," Lo clarified, "but he seemed very pleased with himself."

Isabella thought her brother also looked pleased. Another shot of energy went through her, and she hopped in place a few times. "Oh, my. I cannot believe it." She grabbed both his hands and leaned in close, suppressing a giggle. "We must go and get the letter before the postmaster leaves. It was wise of you to come and fetch me right away."

Lo's smile grew even wider, which Isabella didn't know was even possible. "Yes. I thought you should know right away."

"Come," Isabella directed, releasing his arms but then grabbing one of his hands. She tugged on him, jogging past, and pulled him up the stairs, though he was not resisting. She had to put on her shoes, which she did in a hurry, and threw a shawl around her shoulders before running out the door.

She was too anxious to get the buggy ready, and the postmaster wasn't really that far away.

Lo was behind her as she dashed down the short

pathway to the road out front. She turned to the left and began to run past the long field of green that belonged to a nearby farm. At the end of the road, she would turn right and head straight into town.

Once she was in town, Isabella ran through the alleyway between two buildings and came out on the main road, nearly running into a family who was innocently trying to walk without being run over by anxious women and their brothers.

"Oh," she exclaimed, halting in place and nearly toppling over onto the woman and a child who was between them. She caught herself, though, and thankfully, Lo was able to grab her arm and put her straight back on her feet without issue. She shook her head, giving the family a pleading look. "I am so sorry. Do forgive me. I must slow down."

Neither the man nor the woman gave her a rebuking look. They both smiled at her.

"You see that you do slow down, young lady," the man said gently. "You might hurt yourself running around town like that."

Isabella nodded and gave a short laugh. She tried not to apologize eighty more times but couldn't help repeating it a few more, at least. The family passed.

She glanced at Lo before dashing down the

street toward the post office once again. He was laughing as he followed behind her, reaching out to try to grab her, telling her to slow down.

"I am only walking very fast," she threw over her shoulder, laughing happily. "You have longer legs. I know you can catch up, *mio fratello*."

Flashes of the streets of Portofino made her feel nostalgic, and a wave of melancholy swept over her. She missed her mother and father.

Determined not to let sentiment ruin the moment for her, she pushed that feeling away and headed straight for the postmaster's, lifting her skirt just a bit so she could move faster.

Before going into the small building, though, she took a moment to look around. She didn't see Luke or Dylan or anyone who might tell on her. She pushed the door of the office open and went in backward, smiling at her brother as if he was the reason she'd turned around.

"Ah. Miss Dolly." It was Andrew, the messenger boy, who called her by that name. He was grinning mischievously and came trotting over as soon as Isabella and Lo were inside the building with the door closed. "You've got a letter, Miss *Dolly*." He emphasized the fake name, reaching out to sweep a letter off the desk right behind the counter the office used to serve the public.

He flapped it toward her, coming closer. Isabella felt a giggle inside that made her stomach feel like butterflies had erupted into flight. "I do like that very much," she said, holding out her hand. "And you are a sweet boy for keeping my secret. You tell your boss I said the same about him, too."

"I'll tell him, Miss Isabella. And thank you for the compliment. It... it's nice to hear coming from someone like you."

Isabella tilted her head to the side, examining the boy. She wondered what he meant by that. Should she question him? Would she like his answer?

"I didn't mean nothin' bad by that, Miss Isabella," Andrew said, studying her face. She was amazed by his intuitiveness.

"What did you mean by it, Andrew?" she asked gently.

"Just that... you know... you are..." His cheeks flamed up red, and he ran one hand up and down in front of her. "You're a real pretty lady, you know, and you... you are real nice and... it's just nice that you think of me as your friend. I like that."

Isabella felt affection flood her heart. "Oh, that is

very sweet of you, Andrew," she exclaimed, clutching the letter between her hands in front of her chest. "You are a nice boy and, of course I am friends with you. Thank you for this again." She closed the distance between them and placed a soft kiss on his cheek.

She heard him suck in a sharp breath, and his wide eyes took her in when she leaned back. Giggling, she turned around and gestured with her head to Lo.

"Come on. We better go."

Lo pressed his lips together. She knew he was struggling not to say something silly and sarcastic. He wasn't going to embarrass the boy any more than she already had.

21

Luke rode slowly through town, letting his thoughts wander. He wondered what Isabella would tell him about how to handle Dolly. He'd pondered whether or not to show her the letter, but something was stopping him.

There was something gnawing at him that he couldn't shake. When he'd been writing the letter to Dolly, he'd thought a lot about Isabella. He'd even used her as a reference to decide what he put in the letter. He'd essentially written the letter to Isabella but sent it to Dolly.

He'd put in the letter things he'd tell Isabella if they were closer than just friends. It made him think about the woman in a different light. Now he couldn't shake the feeling of guilt that he'd written a letter to a woman when it should have been given to someone else.

He had already opened the door to Dolly with that letter. It was probably still in the postmaster's office. He had a mind to go and get it back. Maybe he should just give it to Isabella first. Let her read it and get her thoughts on it. That way, he would be able to tell her all the things in the letter without actually *telling* her. It wouldn't look like he was attempting anything more. He was her boss, and he had to respect that. He had no idea if her Italian culture would look down on him if he told her he was attracted to her.

Luke jolted in his saddle when that thought went through his head.

He *was* attracted to her.

But he shouldn't be. He couldn't be. He'd already sent the letter to Dolly.

Luke was brought back to the present when he saw Isabella bolt out from an alleyway and almost run right over an entire family. He snorted with laughter and immediately halted his horse to watch. She apologized profusely, of course. The Wilsons were accommodating, nodding and bowing slightly to her, hurrying their children past her and Lorenzo.

He kept his eyes on the two as they darted across and down the street, excitement glowing from their faces. He enjoyed watching them, delighted by the pair.

Watching them run around like two crazy people was the best entertainment he'd had in a long time. They, too, were going into the postmaster's office, he saw. He decided he would go in afterward and retrieve his letter. No way was he going in there now so they would know why he was there.

He turned his horse in the direction of the barbershop. He had time for a quick trim, and it was decidedly needed. His hair was getting longer than his shoulders, and that was too long, in his opinion. He liked to keep it short enough to manage and long enough to cover his neck during cold winter months. He'd been on too many long runs and knew just how needed that warmth could be.

He glanced over his shoulder once he got to the barbershop, deciding to wait there for the siblings to leave the postmaster. He saw he was in luck when he spotted Dylan inside, sitting in the chair. His friend must have had the same idea.

Luke pushed the door open and went in, looking up at the bell that tinkled over his head.

"Luke." Dylan's eyes swiveled over to him, but he kept his head still.

"Dylan. I see you had the same idea as me."

"Yeah, that's great minds for ya. They think alike, right? Did you take care of all your business in town? What are you doing for dinner? You can eat with us if you like."

"I was thinking I would. I don't have any other plans."

"I want you to come by," Dylan said, following Luke with his eyes as he walked in front of the chair Dylan was sitting in. "I have some news for ya. I think you'll want to celebrate with us."

"News?" Luke's eyebrows shot up. "What kind of news?"

Dylan's grin widened, but he didn't respond. Luke could tell he wanted him to guess. If there was something new and different happening in Dylan's life that Luke didn't know about, it must have had something to do with his wife or the Judge. Since he hadn't heard anything about the Judge or the magazine or anything else, Luke settled on Mattie.

"Is your wife going to have a baby?" he guessed.

Dylan looked like he'd seen a ghost. This time he did move his head, pulling it forward in his shock.

"How did you know that?" he asked in an astonished voice.

Luke laughed. "Process of elimination, my friend. That's exciting. I'm happy for you, I really am."

Dylan closed his eyes for a moment and moved his head back to where it had been. "Sorry bout that," he told the barber, who just nodded with his own grin. "I can't believe you figured it out that fast. That's... that was like lightning speed. I... I really can't believe it."

Luke took a few steps backward until he was against the wall. He leaned back, lifting one leg to put his boot flat against the wall. He crossed his arms over his chest. "I bet you and your little lady are jumping for the moon, ain't ya? Gonna be one good-lookin' kid, I'll tell you what."

"Kind of ya to say so. But that will only happen if the kid looks like Mattie."

"Ain't nothin' wrong with the way you look," Luke stated with a laugh. "And you don't want your boy lookin' like her and your girl lookin' like you, do you? They'll look like themselves."

"They'll be individuals," Dylan added. He stopped himself from nodding and ended up just lifting his chin. "You almost finished there, Herb?"

"Yeap," the barber responded, "Just another..."

He clipped a few more times with his scissors and stepped back. "All done. You can go talk about your baby with Luke movin' your head all ya want."

They laughed as Dylan pulled the bib from around his neck. "Shave another time, then?"

"You bet."

Dylan pulled a coin from his pocket and flipped it to the older man. "Thanks, Herb."

"You bet."

Luke followed Dylan out, glancing down the street as soon as he stepped onto the sidewalk. He didn't see the siblings and had no idea if they'd come back out or not. He hadn't noticed if they'd carried any letters in, but it made him wonder if something exciting was happening with their family in Italy. They appeared to be jumping out of their skin with anticipation.

He wondered if Isabella would tell him what it was all about if he asked her. He wanted to share in the fun. He wanted to be excited and overjoyed with them. He would share Isabella's highs and lows if she let him.

Luke caught himself thinking those thoughts, and it jolted him. He had to get that letter. He could only hope it was still there to be retrieved.

"So we're going to have a party," Dylan said. "And

I know you are invited." His voice brought Luke back to the present. "You find someone you want to bring. Mare, maybe. Someone that will remain a friend since you have Dolly waiting anxiously in New York for your letter."

Luke's stomach turned a bit. He forced a smile. "I'll do my best. You let me know what I can do to help you plan. I'll invite whoever you want me to. We'll talk?" He was moving backward as he spoke, and without waiting for Dylan to respond, he turned and jogged toward the postmaster. He couldn't go through with it. He should have realized before it was Isabella he should have given that letter to.

Luke was relieved when he went into the post office to see it empty of everyone but Andrew, the messenger. He smiled at the young man, feeling a particular fondness for the hard-working kid.

"Howdy, Andrew."

Andrew's eyes were wide. He glanced several times at the front door as if he expected to see someone come in after Luke. Luke just smiled more.

"Was wondering if I could get back that letter I dropped off earlier? I want to make a change to it."

"I, uh, I, uh," Andrew stuttered and stammered, appearing to be at a loss for words. He managed to get himself under control and said, "I'm sorry, Mr.

Turner. The letter already went out with the delivery. The, uh, later delivery that, uh, just left about ten minutes ago."

Luke's heart sank.

"Okay, thank you, Andrew."

He turned away, wondering how he could possibly explain it to Isabella.

Now he had to make a decision.

22

Isabella was taking a chance when she took out the letter from Luke right there in the office, but she couldn't help it. He wasn't there, and she wanted to read it again. He'd been so forthcoming, so gentlemanly and agreeable in the letter.

Really no different from how he was in real life.

She couldn't get past her guilty feelings, however, and it was starting to gnaw at her. One day was all it had been. One day and the urge to confess was so strong, she might have just taken out the letter there in the office on the chance that she would get caught and be forced to admit what she'd done.

When she and Lo had read Luke's letter together

the first time, they'd both been delighted that Luke liked her. The character she'd created was really her—Dolly had her feelings, strengths, weaknesses, knowledge—everything. So she wasn't really lying to him.

Was she?

The letter shook in Isabella's hand, and she hurriedly folded it and tucked it away. He wanted to talk about literature and books. He wanted to talk about the state of the union and the presidency and his business. He wanted to talk about everything, and Isabella was determined to be the one he did that talking to.

She was still debating whether or not she should write him again. It was tempting but would another letter be like the second nail in her coffin? How would he feel when he discovered he'd been deceived and she'd been the one to do it? Would he feel like a fool? Like she had purposefully humiliated and embarrassed him?

Her heart was heavy with these feelings her mind was generating. She almost didn't notice when the door opened.

Luke came in, though, and he was followed by her brother. Seeing the two of them together made

Isabella's heart flutter. Did he know? Had Lo already told him what they'd done?

She studied her brother's face, but he looked happy and calm. There were no storms on his face. In fact, if the way Luke was acting was any indication, he was more than pleased.

Luke slapped one hand on the young man's shoulder, grinning wide at Isabella. "Your brother has an eye for design, Izzie," he said enthusiastically.

Isabella wasn't used to Luke calling her by the shortened version of her name. Tingles erupted over her body when he said it, but she tried not to show her reaction.

"Is that so?" Now she understood why Lo looked so pleased. He had accomplished something and received praise for it. She was anxious to know what it was. "How did you find that out?"

"We were going over some blueprints for the new shed, and he pointed out a few things that will make the design faster and better once it's up. It's not just a simple shed. There's a lot to it, you know. I think he could really make something of himself if he pursues an education in architecture."

Isabella blinked at Luke. "Architecture?" she repeated back to him.

Luke grinned and nodded. "Yes. You know—people who make buildings. Draw the specifics. Floor plans. You know?"

Isabella laughed softly. "Of course I know," she said, shaking her head at him. "I know what an architect is."

"Well, I wasn't sure," Luke murmured, the pleasant look never leaving his face. She liked the way he left his eyes on her when he spoke. It was as if he never wanted to look away. Or maybe that was just her wishful thinking. "Anyway, we have to plan a party for Dylan and Mattie because they are going to have a baby." He said the words slowly and pointedly, his smile growing with every word. "And I am going to be an uncle. Sort of. Maybe a... godfather... I don't know how it works. Either way, I'm gonna be there for the kid through thick and thin."

Isabella loved the way he was talking about his best friend's good news.

"That is very exciting," she gushed, clapping her hands together lightly.

Luke's eyes popped, and he let out a soft laugh. "It is, isn't it?" he exclaimed. "I really never thought this day would come, you know. I've been friends with him for a real long time. He had some thoughts... well, we both had some thoughts that kept us from finding good women in our lives for quite a few years. But along came Mattie and... I haven't seen my friend this happy before. Never. Not even when we bought our first printing press. It was like a baby to us, you know, but what do two bachelors know about having a baby? Nothing. So not the same thing then."

Isabella could tell he was rambling, and she loved it. His bouncy behavior reminded her of the schoolyard when she and the boys used to play. Her upbringing in Italy had been a fine one. She had no complaints.

"You are very happy for him," she noted.

He laughed again. "Can you tell? I just never thought this would happen. Once he married Mattie, sure, I knew it was a possibility and, yeah, that's what happens when people get married, right? They have kids. But to see him as... well, as ecstatic as he is now, his wife, his new ranch, his business that he doesn't have to put any effort into..."

All three laughed.

"No, it doesn't bother me that he isn't working here. He's got a lot on his plate."

"Now, he will have even more. You know he will be terribly worried about them both whenever he isn't on the ranch." Isabella let out a chuckle. "I will bet he will not return to town much anymore at all. He will be too busy taking care of his ranch and his family. We will never see him again unless we go to him."

Luke shared her amusement but shook his head and waved one hand, saying, "Nah, he'll come to town. He'll have to buy supplies for his baby, won't he?"

Their laughter resonated through the building and the door to the printers opened. Penelope emerged, a curious look on her face. "I hear a whole lotta laughter out here," she said, eyeing them all suspiciously. Isabella could see the sparkle behind that look, though.

"Yes, we have been asked to help plan the party for Dylan and Mattie."

Penelope's eyes lit up. "For their new baby. Oh, that will be delightful, I'm sure. I will arrange flowers if you like. I'm personal friends with Lucy at the flower shop."

"That would be so nice," Isabella said as if the offer was for her baby shower and not Mattie's. She closed her mouth and glanced at Luke to see if he objected to her words. His eyes were still on Penelope, and he followed up what she said with his own thoughts.

"Yes, you would be perfect for that arrangement, Penny. You're on top of things like that, aren't you?"

"Yes, sir, I am," Penelope responded proudly.

Luke clapped his hands together. "All right. Let's get to planning."

23

Luke hoped Isabella and Lo didn't think him a fool for his enthusiasm. He'd been trying to think of a reason all night—a reason for him to spend more time with Isabella. Since he couldn't stop the letter from going to Dolly, he'd decided what he was going to do.

All night he'd tossed and turned, trying to figure it out. As a result, he'd come to the press that morning tired. Instead of staying, though, he'd turned and gone on to Dylan's ranch.

That was where he met up with Dylan and Mattie, who were discussing their ideas with Lo— seeing them talking to the young man that way had been a surprise to Luke. But he'd really started when they told him why they were monopolizing the young man's time.

Once they'd established they were going to plan a major event for the announcement of the baby, Luke took Isabella and her brother into his office. He'd put a couch in the room long ago so that Dylan didn't have to sit in a chair and feel like a client when he came to visit Luke. There was a low triple-blown glass coffee table set in front of the long black couch.

Luke went first to his desk, gesturing to the table. "Go ahead and take a seat there. We'll sit down and make a list of things we need for the party and who we want to invite."

Isabella gave him a surprised look. "We're going to invite the guests?" She gave her brother a blank look. "We don't know anyone. Not really. I think Dylan and Mattie will want to make up their own guest list, will they not?"

"They might," Luke said, "but we're going to put down some people just so they aren't forgotten. We don't want to forget anyone, do we?" He shook his head, answering his own question. "No, we don't."

Isabella and Lo sat on the couch. Luke noticed as he pulled open a drawer to retrieve a pad of paper and a pen that they had seated themselves on opposite sides, leaving the middle open for him.

He was happy about that. He knew his observations would be hyper-sensitive now that he'd decided he was interested in Isabella as more than an employee.

Luke was still nervous about how to approach the whole thing. She was such a beautiful woman. Surely she could have any man. He was her boss, and he wasn't sure how she'd feel about that. He'd told himself there was something in the way she looked at him. He really thought he might have a chance with her.

But how he would go about it exactly was still a mystery to him. Until Dolly replied to his letter, he was going to pretend his hadn't even been sent. If and when he got a reply, he would make a decision then. After all, Isabella was right here in Bighorn. Dolly was all the way in New York.

Luke didn't let himself remember that he'd paid for Isabella to come from New York. It hadn't seemed too far away then.

He stepped past Lo's legs as the young man scrunched himself up so Luke could pass and dropped himself in between the siblings. He slapped the notepad on the table and held his pen above it. "All right. Let's make this list."

Luke had been worried the party planning

would be boring. In the end, it turned out he was pretty much right. Isabella stayed in the room only to appease him, he was sure, especially after Lo excused himself and didn't return. He would help out later, he said. There were some tasks he needed to take care of before dark.

Luke felt strange in the pit of his stomach as he watched the young man depart. He was leaving Luke alone in the room with the most beautiful woman he'd ever seen before. A woman he was gradually falling for. Cupid's arrow hadn't yet struck, but Luke felt like the little cherub was hanging around them unseen, biding his time to shoot.

He noticed when Isabella gently moved closer to him and leaned over the list they'd already made. He let his eyes drift to the back of her head so he could admire the waves of brown that flowed freely over her shoulders.

He wanted to touch it. He wanted to plunge his fingers in it and draw her close and kiss her red lips. He felt his skin tingle when she brushed against his thigh as she was moving.

"I think we have covered everything we need to for the party, Luke," she said in a quiet voice, her brown eyes still on the paper. "I simply cannot think of anything we have missed."

Luke almost lost the ability to speak when she glanced back at him.

There it was.

Cupid's arrow.

Luke tried to breathe normally, covering his sudden captivation with nonchalant thoughtfulness. "Yes. You may be right. I... I know I can't think of anything else." *Except you,* he thought immediately after. *Your beauty, your essence, your being.*

Dylan had been the more avid writer between the two of them. Luke had always taken care of the business side of things. It surprised him to have such poetic thoughts. She brought it out in him. She made him a better version of himself. And it had only just started.

Luke recovered and smiled at her. "Shall we take it to Dylan and Mattie now?"

"Surely, they are busy with their daily chores," Isabella replied. He thought about how cute it was for her to be concerned about interrupting their friends.

"No, they'll be close to finished by now. I'm sure Mattie is always willing to talk about anything that has to do with her baby anyway. You just watch. She will be talking about it at every event for the next nine months. Or however long she has left before she births the little thing." He was more than excited about the new life growing in his friend's body. He couldn't wait to see what it looked like and who it would resemble. No matter what, he would have to tease Dylan somehow. Even if the baby didn't have his ears, he would insist it did, but only to elicit a laugh. If the baby really *did* have big ears, he wasn't going to say a word.

"If you believe they will have time for us and don't think we are needed here, then, yes, of course I would like to go with you to the ranch. I'm sure that's where Lo went. He probably had work he had to get back to, and we were distracting him."

Luke laughed. He'd picked up the boy, who'd been in the supply shop buying fishing gear, asking if he wanted to go talk to Isabella for a bit. He hadn't said they were planning to stay for long. Even so, when Lo left the two of them alone, Luke couldn't exactly complain.

He stood up. Gathering all the courage he had in him, he held out his hand to her. She gazed up at him with her big brown eyes, placing her small soft hand into his.

Luke was enthralled by her touch. He wished he could draw her close to him, hug her, envelope her with his warmth, promise her to keep her safe and loved for the rest of her life.

But he held it in. It wasn't the right time. He didn't know when it would be the right time.

It would have to be soon, though. He wouldn't be able to hold back much longer.

24

Isabella was delighted by what she considered their first outing together. She wouldn't let on to how she felt if she could help it, but she had a feeling he was experiencing the same emotions she was. It was something in his eyes, the way he looked at her. Like he never wanted to look away.

She hadn't really seen it until then, and it made her feel a bit breathless. He didn't have to say what he was thinking, not at that moment, anyway. His eyes widened, and it was like he was seeing her for the first time. When he offered her his hand, she took it, expecting and receiving tingles of anticipation.

He let go once they were outside, though, and

the spell was broken. Still, she was left feeling like she was walking on cloud nine. There could be no doubt he was thinking romantic thoughts when he looked at her inside the press office. She was sure she hadn't imagined it.

By the time they got to the restaurant across the street and down one block, she doubted her own memory. Maybe she'd cast those emotions onto him because she was so taken with him. Maybe it had spurned out of her guilt for what she was doing, deceiving him with her letters so he wouldn't be distracted by other women.

She'd even thought a few times about taking his ad out and hoping there weren't too many of the old copies still be sold.

But she couldn't be that manipulative. She would rather just tell him face to face, bluntly, that she was infatuated with him.

Isabella sat down when he pulled out a chair for her and watched as he sat opposite of her.

"The special today is beef stew," he said. "It's really good, but on hot days like today, I prefer the cold cuts. Sandwiches and maybe just a small bowl of soup or stew. I don't make it my main course or anything."

Isabella nodded, her eyes still on his handsome

face. He was speaking so casually as if they were married and had been together for years. She heard the familiarity of her father's tone when he spoke to her mother.

"I have never really thought about it," she said, "but your strategy sounds logical to me."

He smiled at her. "What part of Italy are you from?" he asked curiously.

Isabella hesitated before she answered. She tilted her head slightly and gave him a soft look. "Do you know anything about Italy?" she asked.

His cheeks flushed. She hadn't meant to embarrass him, but it was clear she had. She spoke quickly to make up for it.

"I am sure you have seen in on a globe." She lifted her hands and made the shape of the small country. "This is the top and this is the bottom and this is where my little village of Portofino is located." She stabbed the air toward the bottom of her imaginary map of Italy. "Not many people are aware of its existence. It is a wonder that my father found it. Not so much a wonder that he stayed."

"If your mother is anything like you," Luke stated gently, "I can really understand why he stayed."

"It is a beautiful village," Isabella continued, not acknowledging what he'd said. Her mind filled with moving images, memories of her childhood, running the streets of Portofino with her best friend, Bianca, collecting rocks and searching for little critters to take home to show their brothers. "Many people are visiting now, but not when I was growing up. I believe my father had something to do with that. He..." She lifted her hands in the air and made finger quotes, "put our village on the map, as they say."

Luke nodded. "He had a lot of friends here in the states, then?"

"When he was a young man at the academy, he was very popular," Isabella responded, recalling several stories in her mind her father had told her about his days as a youth. "When he traveled the world as a young man, he came upon Portofino with no intention of remaining there. But he fell in love with the countryside and with my mother. So he stayed. He has never forgotten this great country, though, and encouraged us to visit from the time we were very young."

"That's real nice to hear," Luke said. "I can't imagine leaving and never coming back. Does he plan to ever return?"

Isabella felt a touch of sadness in her heart and shook her head. "No, there is little for him here.

Although, now that Lo and I are here, perhaps he will come to visit if we decide to stay for good."

Luke looked like she'd hit him with a block of wood. He sat back, staring at her. "You aren't planning to stay? I thought you'd moved to the states."

Isabella's expression didn't change. She shrugged. "We may or may not. We had not decided on either way. I would like to stay. Lo would like to stay. So..." She shrugged again. "We will probably stay."

She saw the relief on his face. He was about to speak when a girl came over to the table to get their orders. She deferred to Luke, and he ordered for the two of them.

"Thanks, Becky," he said as the girl turned away. She smiled at him. He averted his eyes to Isabella, his easy grin remaining. "She's a nice girl."

Isabella nodded, watching the young woman disappear through the kitchen door. "She reminds me of my best friend when I was growing up." She leaned forward on the table, resting her arms in front of her to hold her up. The table was cold but soon warmed up underneath her skin. "There was this old woman who lived on the edge of Portofino in this little house, a shack, really. She was not ever married that I heard of. She had no children ever. As children, you know we thought of her as a witch. We thought she put spells on people, and for a time, I even thought she could heal the sick. I remember wondering if she could bring back those who had died."

Luke lifted his eyebrows. "But she wasn't a witch?"

Isabella laughed softly. "No, of course she wasn't. She was a medicine woman. She was a healer. She made potions from herbs and used them to treat people who were ill. I did not find that out until I myself became sick, and it was she who treated me and made sure I did not die."

"Huh. That's pretty amazing. I'm glad she was able to save you. Were you friends with her after that?"

"We were not afraid of her anymore, I can say that," Isabella replied, nodding. She remembered the last time she'd visited the woman. "The last time I visited her, she was not doing well herself. I should not be surprised since she was likely a hundred years old by that time."

"How long ago was that?"

Isabella had to think. She lifted her eyes as if the answer was drifting in the air around her. "Oh, I would say about four years. I was just turning twenty, and she wanted to wish me a happy birthday. My father took me by to say hello and wish her well. She gave me a potion. She said it relieves headaches, which it has done since then. I still have some left." She was fully aware of the pride in her voice. It was a point of pride to her that she'd been able to keep the medicine for that long.

"I hope it still works the same. Sometimes age causes things like that to lose potency."

Isabella blinked at him. He laughed and shrugged. "Just something I heard."

25

―――――

Isabella thought about that lunch while she set out plates for the party. She was a guest of Dylan and Mattie, and they'd already jumped on her once for doing the staff's job, but she was eager to help out. It was in her nature.

The party would soon be in full swing. There was a man playing guitar already and singing songs Isabella had never heard before. She liked them, though, and found herself humming along once she caught the tune.

She was excited. Not just because she always enjoyed a good party and since coming to America, Dylan's parties had far surpassed any she'd attended in Italy, but also because Luke would be there front and center. It had been a week since their first outing together. They had talked during that time but hadn't shared any more intimate moments. Not like that lunch.

Isabella longed to experience it again. She wanted to be across from him, laughing, talking, gazing into his incredible eyes.

"You must be patient," she murmured to herself, leaving her eyes on the plates she'd just set down. "He will be here soon enough."

"Izzie." She looked up when she heard Mattie's voice call out her name. She smiled brightly, feeling the warmth of affection flow through her as the woman came down the grassy slope toward her. "I see you are doing work again. Will you stop that." Mattie laughed, closing the distance with one hand stretched out toward Isabella.

Isabella stepped away from the table, laughing. When Mattie was close enough, Isabella took her friend's hand and allowed herself to be pulled back up the hill toward the main house.

"Everyone of note is inside the house," Mattie said exuberantly. She glanced over her shoulder, meeting Isabella's eyes. "You want to see Luke, don't you?"

A tingle of apprehension slid through Isabella's

chest. She balked before saying, "Y... yes, I suppose I do."

Mattie laughed delightedly. "No need to be shy around me, Izzie. I've been waiting a long time for that man to find himself a good woman. I've seen the way you two look at each other. It's clear you want to be together. So what's stopping you? Why all the cat-footing around?"

Isabella pulled her eyebrows together. "I do not understand the term cat-footing. I have never heard it before."

Mattie stopped pulling on her, and they stood near the house, face to face. Mattie looked so excited. It was contagious. Isabella could feel her friend's energy spilling over into her. She had to admit it was a nice feeling. She liked it very much.

Mattie clapped her hands together, her face bright and glowing as she spoke. "You two are good for each other, and you won't ever realize it if you keep pretending it's not there. I've spoken to Luke, and I think he agrees with me. You should spend as much time as you can with him tonight and see if he gets up the courage to tell you how he really feels. I bet you he would if you gave him a little nudge."

When she said the last few words, she jutted out

her elbow and tapped Isabella with it, a mischievous look on her face.

"You know you want to," she urged Isabella with a soft laugh.

"I... I suppose I do feel something for Luke," Isabella said, dropping her volume and looking around her cautiously. "But he is my boss. I do not know if such a thing is ethical."

"Ethical schmethical," Mattie replied dismissively, waving one hand in the air. "When you fall in love with someone, it doesn't matter what job they have. You're in love. You have to pursue it. Just ask my father." She winked at Isabella. "He's a judge. He has seen it all. Put you and Luke in the same room with him for an hour, and he'll be able to tell you if it's the real thing."

Isabella felt a little overwhelmed by her friend's enthusiasm. She wasn't so sure. Not yet. She could tell Luke was interested in her, and she definitely reciprocated that feeling. But they were still on edge, not quite at the point where they felt comfortable being open with each other.

It was something Isabella was looking forward to. But despite Mattie's apparent confidence, Isabella wasn't there yet.

"You have the comfort of already being married,"

she said, hoping her words weren't taken the wrong way. "Surely you remember when you and Dylan were not yet together, and you were unsure what your next step should be."

Mattie's eyes moved back and forth quickly. Isabella could tell she was remembering her own past with Dylan. She had no idea how the two had gotten together, but she figured it must have been something adventurous. That was Mattie and Dylan to a tee. They were exuberant, energetic go-getters, always on the move, always accomplishing something new.

Luke ran at a different pace. She could already tell he was more laid back and wasn't pressing to do more work than he already had to do. He wasn't lazy. He just wasn't consumed with tasks he put upon himself. Mattie and Dylan obviously loved that lifestyle.

Isabella was glad Luke didn't run at that fast pace.

"Listen, I was wondering if you would do me a favor," Mattie resumed her fast walking and talking, Isabella in tow.

"I will certainly try. What is it?"

Mattie grinned. "I want to learn Italian. Will you teach me Italian?"

Isabella laughed. "I would love to have someone besides Lo to speak the language with. Yes, I would be delighted to teach it to you."

Mattie clapped her hands happily. "Oh, thank you. Come on, let's get inside. Don't worry. We'll all be back out here to enjoy the beautiful day real soon."

ISABELLA'S STOMACH WAS FULL. She had eaten more than her fair share, she supposed, and would now have to occupy the chair she was in for at least a few more minutes before she could take her plate to the garbage bin. She would probably pick up a few more on the way from guests who had left their plates behind. That was her style. She might get a hard look from Mattie, but she would do it anyway.

She could see Mattie's "hard look" in her mind and had to laugh softly. She'd been receiving that look all evening. Now, as the party was winding down to a close and the sun was beginning to set, there was even more opportunity for Mattie to scold her. She didn't mind helping to clean up, even if Mattie and Dylan were paying people to do it.

Isabella looked around at the remaining guests.

It had been a lovely party. The guitar player had been joined by others who brought their instruments, and they ended up with a makeshift band, who played bouncy songs for people to dance to. She'd had the prime opportunity to dance with Luke and took full advantage of it, though he really was quite stiff the whole time, she had to admit.

Nothing like Mattie and Dylan, who had flailed their bodies all around in stylish coordination. Luke looked embarrassed the whole time his rigid body moved from side to side. There was no swaying where Luke was concerned. It was a little surprising, considering he was a very outgoing man otherwise.

He'd been giving her that "look" all night, too—the opposite of Mattie's teasing scowl.

She pushed herself to her feet and took in a deep breath, turning around to pick up her plate.

Her body erupted in chills when a hand slid around hers and stopped her from picking up the plate. She felt a body directly behind her as the person leaned over and whispered in her ear.

She closed her eyes and took in Luke's words, feeling the softness of his breath on her ear.

"No cleaning right now. Come with me."

26

Luke had been waiting all night for the right time to say something to Isabella. She looked so beautiful, even though she was dressed casually. He'd consulted Dylan, who'd encouraged him to go for it. He said it was about time Luke buckled down and let the woman know how he was feeling.

It would still be a week before he would receive any letters from New York. He'd discreetly removed his ad from the next issue of their magazine. Sometimes he wished he could remove it from the old magazines, as well.

He would just have to tell the sweet Dolly that he had chosen another. There was no denying it now.

He was in love with Isabella. Waiting any longer to tell her seemed pointless.

He could tell how surprised she was by the way he'd approached her in the party tent. He'd wanted to make the maximum effect and felt like he'd accomplished that when he saw her bright face. Her brown eyes were so wide. Her lips slightly parted in surprise. How he longed to kiss them.

Soon, he told himself. Soon.

They were standing face to face with only a foot or so between them, and he lifted his hand, his eyes on hers.

"Come for a walk with me?" he asked in a soft, low voice. "I think we should talk."

Isabella nodded without saying a word. She put her hand in his.

Luke's heart beat hard as they walked out of the tent and out toward the huge flower garden behind one side of Dylan's ranch. He didn't know exactly where to start or what to say. Dylan was the wordsmith. He found himself wishing he'd asked his friend for the right words.

Then again, they wouldn't have been *his* words. He never wanted to be anything less than honest with Isabella. She deserved the best.

"I hope I didn't scare you, pulling you away from

the party like that," he said, deciding to just say whatever came to his mind. He had to relax around her. Otherwise, he wouldn't be authentic, and he wanted desperately to be open with her.

"You did not scare me," she replied. He heard the softness of her voice, and it made his stomach explode with butterflies. "I was delighted that you asked me to go on a walk." To his surprise and delight, she placed her hand on her stomach, shaking her head, and went on, "I believe I ate too much, and now my stomach is so very full. Walking will help me relieve some of that pressure. This is what my mother told me."

Luke nodded. "I find exercise and walking to be wonderful after a big meal."

They were quiet for a few moments, entering the garden through a black iron gate. There were large bushes all around that made a sort of maze around the flowerbeds. It would only serve as a true maze to small children, though, because none of the bushes were higher than Luke's chest. At one point, the bushes were trimmed to waist high. A child could jump and see their way out.

In the very middle of the unique garden were four benches creating a square, placed on top of solid, flat ground. They surrounded a thick, tall tree, the tallest of all the trees on the land. Probably the oldest, as well. Its branches spread out fifteen feet in all directions, creating the largest shade tree Luke had ever seen.

"This is such a lovely garden," Isabella murmured, looking around. "I think that every time I come here."

"Have you walked through often?"

Isabella shook her head. "A few times with Mattie. She is grateful to Dylan for creating this for her. It is her favorite spot to sit when she needs to be calm and peaceful for a while." She giggled and continued on, much to Luke's surprise. She sounded so casual and comfortable with him. And that was exactly what he wanted. "I was thinking before the party that Mattie and Dylan are very excitable people. They are ready for adventure all the time. I'm not like that. I don't think you are either."

She looked up at him and grabbed his heart with her eyes. He resisted the urge to pull her into a kiss.

"I wouldn't shy away from adventure," he pointed out, "but I am definitely not out seeking it like those two. You are right about that. I don't really see you as being that way either, though you did take quite a risk traveling all the way from Italy and then coming from New York to here just because you were offered the chance."

Isabella headed toward the benches under the shade tree, so Luke naturally followed along behind her, admiring her shape as her hips swayed when she walked. "It is actually different," she responded, dropping on one of the benches, looking up at him expectantly. He sat next to her and gazed at her while she spoke, enjoying every word that came from her mouth.

"How is that?" he asked.

"Because Lo and I prepared for this one thing, this one adventure for a long time. All our lives, really. And we did not seek out any other adventure. We were simply making a change in our lives. A change that was encouraged by my father from the time we were little children. You asked me if I thought my papa would visit America again. I said I did not know, but I do know. It was not my intention to lie. My father will visit. He will come, and maybe he will stay if my mama also wants to. My father was the man for a life like that. I and my brother and mother are not."

"I see."

He was going to continue, but there was a look in

Isabella's eyes that told him she wanted to tell him something. He waited.

"If... if you had the chance, would you visit Italy?" she asked slowly.

Luke hadn't expected the question, but once it was asked, he was flooded with the prospects of what that meant. He studied her face. "With you?" he asked as casually as he could.

She must have been as determined as he was not to lose her cool. She nodded, her face never changing, her eyes never leaving his.

"Yes," he answered bluntly. "If I was with you, I would visit Italy."

The look that came over her face made Luke's heart thump hard. Her gaze softened, and it seemed her body relaxed completely. He hadn't even realized how tense she was until her shoulders slumped just a little, and she seemed to shrink slightly.

"Isabella, I have to tell you something." He had to get it out. He had to let her know what was in his heart. He had no patience left. It was time to confess.

Isabella blinked at him rapidly. He could see her chest rising and falling faster. She was as nervous as he was. All he had to do was tell her. Just open his mouth and let the words spill out.

He steadied his nerves. He took a moment. She

continued to sit there, right in front of him, in all her beauty, expectant for the words he felt she wanted to hear. She felt the same about him as he felt about her. He just had to remember that.

"I have fallen in love with you," he said, a surge of adrenaline striking him like lightning as he said it, "and I'm hoping you feel the same way about me."

27

Isabella felt like she might faint. But there was no way she was going to let that happen when she heard the words she so desperately wanted to hear. He was telling her he loved her. He had fallen in love with her.

She hardly knew how to respond. She was bursting with love for him, but her mind was blank when she opened her mouth to speak.

Isabella knew she needed to keep herself as calm as possible and act like a mature adult about this. But she wanted to jump up and down and do cartwheels and throw her arms around him and dance the night away.

She forced herself, though trembling, to be calm

as she replied in the softest voice, "I have fallen in love with you, too."

Luke immediately sucked in a deep breath and let it out loudly, closing his eyes momentarily. He leaned toward her, his arms outstretched. For a moment, she was unsure what he was about to do. But he pulled her into a warm hug, and it felt perfect to her. He hadn't taken it too far. He hadn't made her feel uncomfortable. Far from it, the feelings she was having were pleasant. Her body tingled. Her heart sang with joy. Her mind raced with anticipation.

"I can't tell you how glad I am that we feel the same way," he murmured into her hair. "I didn't know how to say it. I've been so worried that you would think because I am your boss that I was pushing myself on you. I don't want to be aggressive with you, Izzie. I want to be gentle and kind and loving with you."

He pulled back and looked into her eyes. She felt like she could see into his soul. He was so perfect for her. She couldn't stop thinking about it. Listening to his outpouring of emotion, she knew she had done the right thing making the trip to America. Her father had encouraged it for so long. She hadn't understood why for many years. She'd thought for a time he just wanted to get rid of her and her brother.

But now she understood. He knew there was much more to life and to the world than the tiny village of Portofino.

"I want to be the one to wake you up with breakfast in bed." Luke offered, his smooth voice penetrating her mind and filling her heart with love. "I want to buy you nice things and protect you from danger. I don't want you to depend on anyone else. Not even yourself."

"Lo might object to that," Isabella remarked with a giggle. "He had always been the one to protect me."

"I'm sure he won't mind if I take over," Luke responded, smiling. "Especially when he finds out my feelings for you are pure and genuine. I have never felt this way before, Izzie. I can honestly say that. I know I must seem old to you—"

"I don't know how old you are," she interjected.

He narrowed his eyes. "I'm older than you," he said mysteriously. "Let's just leave it at that for now."

Isabella laughed. She could already tell she was going to have fun with Luke. He had a good sense of humor. "I'm going to find out eventually, you know. How will I throw you a birthday party if I do not know when your birthday is or how old you are?"

Luke shrugged, putting on a serious expression

that Isabella could easily see through. "I reckon you'll just have to guess. Or make every day my birthday." He looked thoughtful. "I wouldn't mind that. A birthday cake every day? Seems like a good idea to me."

Isabella gasped and swatted at him with one hand. "Sounds like a very fattening idea to me. I should not do that to you or to anyone I love."

They both laughed.

Isabella couldn't believe how comfortable she felt. Now that she knew he felt the same way as she did, she felt different even looking at him. There was a new connection to him when her eyes met his, the beginning of what she knew would be an unbreakable bond.

He had turned to the side and put one hand on the back of the bench. The smile on his face was pure delight. She thought he looked even more handsome than he had just five minutes previous. Living the rest of her life waking up to him in the morning was going to be amazing.

"Anyway, I'll continue now, if that's okay." He raised his eyebrows as if asking her permission, his eyes sparkling with excitement. She giggled and nodded. He pulled in another deep breath. "I know

I'm older than you, and I've been around plenty of women. There are some here in Bighorn that would fall over backward if I would give them a chance. But you know I never felt a connection to them. No pull toward them. Not like... not as I do with you."

Isabella let herself feel a modicum of jealousy that there were women in their hometown that were interested in Luke. Of course there had to be. How could there not? She didn't want to know who they were. She would let that fact slide through her mind and disappear into the recesses of things she didn't want to remember.

"I don't want you to ever think I don't care about you... that I don't... love you." He said the last two words like he was trying on a new hat. "I know I do. There can't be anything else that feels like this." His eyes were intense. She felt her body heating up as he spoke. "I... think about you. All the time. All day and night. I wonder what you're doing. If you're okay and happy. If you're safe. You're usually safe. I don't worry about that much." He grinned, and she let out a soft laugh.

"You provided that big house," she remarked. "I am very safe."

Luke nodded. "I am so glad I let you stay there.

I'm glad you felt safe there. I want you to come to depend on me. For anything and everything. All you have to do is ask, and I'll do whatever I can to see you get what you want."

Isabella remembered the short passage in Dylan's journal about his friend and how lonely he was. She would not take advantage of Luke's soft heart. She would not be a greedy woman, asking for everything under the sun.

Her thoughts led her to shake her head, which caused a look of alarm to come to Luke's face.

"No, no," she said quickly, "I do not shake my head to say no to you. I am refusing to become a needy woman, a greedy woman. I will not take advantage of your love and your kind heart, Luke. We will be partners, you and I. We will work together and protect each other and take care of each other."

His relief was obvious. The tension left his shoulders, and he relaxed.

"You are a wonderful woman, Isabella. I don't want to spend another day without you. Will you marry me?"

Isabella's heart nearly exploded. She pressed her hands together in front of her lips, tears filling her eyes. She nodded, swallowing hard so she could get the words out. "Yes, Luke. I will marry you."

His arms were around her the next moment. She relaxed against him, closing her eyes and absorbing his loving words as he cried out softly into her hair, "Thank God. Thank God."

28

———

Isabella was stunned when Luke suddenly pulled back and grabbed her upper arms with his strong hands.

"That's it," he exclaimed. She blinked at him, her eyes wide. "That's it. Come on. Come with me. I have to... I have to get it for you."

Adrenaline shot through her when he jumped to his feet and pulled her up with him. She grabbed her skirt so she wouldn't trip as they ran back toward the ranch house. There weren't many guests left, and the sun had gone down, so the only light came from the moon—which was fairly bright—and the lanterns placed all around the grounds.

She could see well enough, though, and ran up the porch steps behind him. He was kind enough not to yank on her hand, as his legs were much longer, and he could have gone faster if he didn't have hold of her hand.

Isabella wasn't sure she would have cared either way. He could drag her across the floor if he wanted to, as long as he didn't let go of her hand. It felt too good. Just knowing he was in love with her made her feel like she could fly with wings on her feet.

Thinking this made her even more energetic.

When they got inside, she expected him to head toward the den, where everyone who was left from the party, including Dylan and Mattie. But Luke pulled her in another direction, and they headed down one of the hallways toward the other parts of the house.

Luke stopped in front of a narrow door that Isabella thought could only be going down into a cold cellar or a basement. It looked like one of those doors. She gave Luke a curious look. He faced her and spoke in a low voice.

"I have a lot of boxes down there in the basement —boxes from my childhood, my family, that kind of thing. I want to find something that's in those boxes. Do you want to come down and search with me, or would you rather stay up here and wait for me?"

The first thing that came to Isabella's mind was

that she didn't want to be away from Luke. She didn't care if she was in a dark, dusty basement with him or a king's palace. She just knew she wanted to be with him. Forever and always.

"I'll go down with you and help you search," she answered, taking both his hands in hers and looking directly into his eyes, "but you have to tell me what we're searching for."

He laughed with delight. "We're looking for a jewelry box. It's about this big." He held his hands out and moved them to make a square about seven inches from side to side. It has a small rectangle of colored glass in the middle of the lid. It's thick, at least, it looks thick, but there's actually room for quite a lot of jewelry in there."

Isabella was amused by his excited, child-like tone. She suspected the jewelry box was his mother's, and it was reminding him of growing up.

"It's dark-colored," he said, finally turning to the narrow door and grabbing the knob. "And I don't think we'll have a hard time finding it."

As she followed him down the steps, holding onto his shoulder, though he was holding a lantern high on full beam so she could see well where she was going, she asked, "Why are your things here and

Dylan's things at the other house? I'm surprised you brought anything here."

He glanced over his shoulder at her as he took the last step onto the ground. "That's a long story. I was going to get the ranch. He was going to run the magazine. He's the writer, you know. As events played out, it went the opposite way, and he ended up married and wanting to be settled. No more traveling for the magazine or advertising or any of that. Now that he's starting a family, that life is long gone. I'd already started moving in when things changed."

Isabella breathed in and immediately choked on a bit of dust floating through the air. She coughed and waved one hand in front of her nose. "Oh my," she said when she recovered, noticing Luke had stood by her, watching with concerned eyes. He set the lantern on a tall counter behind him and took her by the shoulders.

"You all right?" he asked in a worried tone.

"I'm... I'm all right, yes. Sorry."

Luke shook his head, a regretful look on his face. "Don't be sorry. I'm sorry I brought you down here into this dusty basement. But I really think you'll like the reason I did it."

Isabella had a sneaking suspicion she knew why he wanted the jewelry box. She nodded, returning his grin with one of her own. She hoped he could see how much she cared for him, even in the dim light of the lantern.

"So, where do we start looking first?" she asked. "I do not want to stay down here any longer than we have to." She rubbed her arms with her hands. "It is very chilly."

"You're right," Luke stated firmly. "It's miserable down here. Let's see, right over here, these are my things."

"These are all belongings from your childhood?" she asked, lifting her eyes and trying to see what the shapes of the shadows might represent. When he held up the lantern, he revealed an entire house worth of furniture.

"Yes, these are things from my parents' house."

She heard a note of pain in his voice and didn't want to bring any negativity to their thoughts, so she turned the topic back to the jewelry box. "Where do you think the box is? Do you know?"

Luke's attention focused back on what they were doing, which was exactly what Isabella wanted to happen. Satisfied that she'd averted a possible emotional disaster, she followed him as he made a line for a dresser backed against a wall.

He held the lantern out to her without saying a

word, and she took it, her eyes still on the dresser. He pulled open the top drawer and shuffled through the papers and other contents. Shaking his head, he closed it and opened the second drawer.

"I know I kept it in here for safekeeping," he mumbled. Isabella ran her eyes from one side of the drawer to the other. When he pushed some papers aside, she saw dark brown wood and grabbed his arm with her hand. "I think I saw it. Is that it?"

She reached in front of him and moved the papers back out of the way, revealing a dark wood box with a small rectangle of colored glass in the middle of the lid. She turned her head to Luke, smiling wide.

"Well, I'll be," he exclaimed. "That was fast. Thank you. You must really want to get out of this basement."

Isabella laughed. "I did not do that on purpose. But yes, we should go now that we have found it. This place is so dark and dusty. And cold. Let us go back upstairs."

He nodded, took her hand, and hurried back to the stairs.

Isabella was relieved by the warmth of the first floor, glad when he closed the door to the damp basement.

Instead of standing there to examine the jewelry box and its contents, he immediately took her hand again and pulled her to a door on the other side of the hallway. Isabella recognized the library where she and Luke had stood once before and talked. He didn't stay in the room, though. He continued to the double glass doors. Letting go of her hand, he opened the door and ushered her through.

"It is warmer outside than it is in that basement," he said, taking the lantern from her and placing it on a table on the veranda where they now stood, underneath a moon that was nearly full, but not quite.

Isabella felt overwhelmed when he stood in front of her, facing her, the jewelry box between them. He opened it and withdrew a ring with a prominent diamond surrounded by green gems.

"I hope this fits you," he murmured.

Isabella's heart quaked. Fresh tears rose to her eyes and spilled over. She covered her mouth with one hand and held the other one out to him.

Luke put the box on the table next to the lantern and took her hand in his.

"God, please make Izzie's finger the same size as my momma's," Luke whispered. She looked up and noticed he had closed his eyes. He was actually praying. He opened his eyes and met her with them.

Without looking down, he slid the ring onto her finger.

It felt cold for only a moment. When Isabella realized it was a perfect fit, she was elated.

They both gave each other excited looks and met together in a laughing hug that made Isabella think that she and Luke, like the ring, were also a perfect fit.

29

Isabella glanced in the mirror when the door opened, and Mattie came back through. She'd only left a moment before to get some sewing supplies from the closet in the hallway. She was fussing over the sash on Isabella's dress. It wasn't perfect, and it had to be perfect, as far as Mattie was concerned.

She smiled wide.

"What are you doing, Mattie? You do not need to be so frantic."

Mattie stopped and stared at Isabella, blinking quickly. "I am not being frantic, Isabella Russo. You take that back."

Isabella laughed, looking at her reflection once again. It was the day of her wedding. Luke was waiting for her under the same party tent at Dylan's ranch that might as well stay standing year-round as much as they used it.

She and Luke had waited two months. That was enough time to plan something nice and to have Mr. and Mrs. Russo travel from Italy to see their daughter get married. They planned to stay a month.

Thinking about their arrival in Bighorn made Isabella want to cry. She'd been so happy she could have done cartwheels for miles. She didn't realize just how much she missed them until she saw them. There had been many hugs. They had both loved Luke the moment they laid eyes on him.

"I am teasing you," Isabella said to comfort her good friend. Mattie had been responsible for much of the decorations and other pleasantries at the wedding ceremony. It was her home, and she knew how to decorate it. That's what she'd told Isabella anyway.

"I just want it all to be so nice, so right," Mattie went on, coming over to pin the sash to Isabella's dress. She had a needle in her mouth, string curling from one end of it, floating in the air as Mattie moved.

Two minutes later, the sash was sewn on the

dress, and Isabella was turning side to side, examining it.

"I just can't believe it had to come off the day of the wedding," Mattie complained, frowning.

"Do not worry, Mattie," Isabella responded, trying to stay positive. "At least it happened before, so I would not be walking down the aisle with my sash hanging down to my ankles."

Mattie cheered up, and they both laughed. "You are a delight, Izzie," Mattie complimented her, coming over to stand next to her friend at the full-length mirror. They looked at their reflections. "I prayed for you, you know. I mean, I prayed that Luke would find a good woman. He and Dylan were so close. I know it had to make him feel lonely when Dylan moved on with me."

Isabella nodded, remembering the journal passage where Dylan had said something akin to his wife's words. "Yes, I feel he has been lonely without his best friend, as well. But he will never be lonely again. I will not let that happen."

Mattie's smile stretched from ear to ear. She moved her eyes to Isabella's reflection as she wrapped one arm around her friend's shoulders. "I'm so happy you came to Bighorn," she gushed, her voice rising up several octaves. "We are going to make two very happy families."

Isabella returned Mattie's smile. "*Hai praticato il tuo italiano?*" She asked Mattie if she had been practicing her Italian. The two had grown close while Mattie helped Isabella prepare for the wedding, and Isabella had been more than happy to begin teaching her Italian.

Mattie's grin grew wider. Isabella thought her cheeks would soon start to hurt, just as her own would by the end of the day, she was sure.

"*Si, un po,*" Mattie replied, holding up her thumb and index finger to indicate she had been practicing but only a little. She moved away from Isabella so she could stand back and survey the whole look.

Isabella laughed. "I am delighted that you understood what I asked you. You are coming along nicely. Soon we will have long conversations in Italian, and our men will stand by wondering what we are saying."

Mattie joined her laughter. "They will think we are talking about them," she exclaimed.

"Oh, yes, I am sure they will. And perhaps we might be doing just that."

Their light laughter continued.

"But Lo will tell them what we are really saying if

he is around," Mattie said. "I suspect your brother would not want them to feel bad thinking we are talking about them."

Isabella looked at Mattie in the mirror again. "I guess I would not want them thinking we are saying bad things. I would not say bad things. Luke is a good man. A gentleman. So generous and kindhearted. He is just the kind of man my father wanted me to marry."

Mattie nodded, her eyes soft with affection. "Yes, he is. He and Dylan are both the best of men. We are so blessed. So lucky. Both of us. I'm so happy for you, Izzie. I'm so glad we will be related in a way."

Isabella's heart filled with affection for the woman. She was about to respond when the door behind her opened, and Lo bounded in like a puppy dog off a leash.

"It's time," he announced breathlessly.

Isabella had to take a moment to look at her brother, who was dressed in a fine shirt and new trousers. Even his shoes were polished to a shine. His hair was slicked back, revealing just how handsome he really was when he cleaned himself up.

"Lo. What a handsome young man you are." Isabella twirled around and grabbed her brother in a tight, loving hug. "I am ready. Are you ready?"

Lo was going to be leading her down the aisle while her father was on her other side. The two most important men in her life would be giving her away to the one who would be her husband, her protector, for the rest of her life.

"Papa is anxious to walk down the aisle with you," Lo said with a laugh. She knew he had heard her compliment. As usual, he took it in stride. He was a fine young man. She would have to see if she could find him a good woman, maybe through an ad in a magazine.

Her thoughts made her giggle uncontrollably. She, Mattie, and Lo left the room in a hurry. Mattie caught her giggling fit, and they squeezed each other's hands as they went down the hallway behind Lo.

"It's time." Lo said when they reached the front door. "Everyone will be watching you from here on. Are you ready?"

"I am ready," Isabella announced, pulling up to stand straight and tall, even though her knees were as weak as a newborn lamb's.

Luke was so excited, his skin was tingling and his heart was fluttering in his chest. He was standing at the altar, waiting for Isabella to come around the corner of the house and head toward the outdoor shelter. He resisted the urge to chew on his lip. He wanted to appear calm and collected.

It was just another day, right? Everyone got married. This was normal—nothing to be anxious about.

He lifted one shoulder and then the other, shifting the jacket that suddenly seemed itchy to him. He put one finger inside his tie and loosened it, wondering why he'd tied it so tight.

"Calm down, Luke," Dylan whispered from

beside him. He glanced over and saw the highly amused look on his friend's face.

"You calm down," Luke replied. "You're not the one getting married. "

"I know," Dylan retorted, clearly entertained by Luke's anxiety. "I got married already. I lived through it just fine. You're sweating bullets. Calm down. This isn't the end of the world, you know."

Luke saw the amusement in the situation and grinned at his friend, who returned it fully.

His anxiety dissipated the moment Isabella rounded the corner, her brother escorting her. Mattie was in front of her now, holding a pretty yellow bouquet of flowers. Isabella's flowers were also yellow, with a smattering of tiny red ones throughout the bouquet. Luke was impressed with the angelic portrait Isabella made. She was so incredibly beautiful. He didn't know how he could have gotten so lucky.

"Look at her," he exclaimed under his breath to Dylan.

"Shut up, you idiot," Dylan murmured back. "This is a wedding."

Luke struggled not to laugh at his friend's response, having to cough to cover it up. He lifted one fist in front of his mouth and did his best to get himself under control. He cleared his throat and sniffed, turning his gaze to the preacher, who looked even more amused than Dylan.

Soon, Isabella was standing by his side. She'd chosen a veil that came down only halfway so he could see her lips but only the outline of her eyes through the fabric. He was happy when she was standing in front of him so he could lift it and take in the loving gaze she was giving him.

Luke couldn't imagine living a day in his life without this woman. She had taken up residence in his heart and was never going to leave it. He would protect her and everything and everyone she loved for the rest of his life.

He said his vows with vehemence and truthfulness, keeping his eyes on hers the whole time. When she responded with hers, he drank in the words, vowing to remember that moment until his dying day.

When the ceremony was over, Dylan had paid the boys attending the wedding to clear out the chairs, altar, and decorations to make way for the tables and chairs for the reception. Dylan had offered to put up two tents, one for the ceremony and one for the reception, but Luke had said it was unnecessary. It would save money to have the boys just move the chairs. Plus, they'd get paid for it, and that was their favorite thing in the world.

While the boys were clearing the way, most of the ladies went inside the house and retrieved the food they had brought with them. They would bring it out and coordinate it on the tables, so anyone who wanted to eat could do so when they wanted. The men and children scattered around the backyard, the men talking, the children playing.

Luke and Isabella were left on their own for a time. Luke had planned a walk along the winding river that cut through part of Dylan's land. It was a ten-minute walk to reach the edge of the water.

"We don't have to stay there if you don't want to," he said as they walked, hand in hand, as husband and wife, down the path that cut through the woods. "We don't even have to go on this walk if you don't want to. Whatever you want to do, Izzie, you just tell me. I'll do it. Whatever you want."

She smiled at him, turning her gaze to meet his. He wondered how long it would be before he ceased to be amazed at her beauty. He would never tire of it, he was sure of that. He would love her and consider her beautiful when her hair turned gray and her face was wrinkled with age. If there was one thing he was completely sure of, it was that he wanted to grow old with her. There would never be another woman in his life that would make him feel the way Isabella did.

"I like this walk," she responded softly, moving closer to him so she could rest her head on his shoulder. They were walking slowly. There was no rush.

He let his eyes roam around, taking in their surroundings with elated eyes. It was like he was seeing trees and bushes and flowers and squirrels for the first time. Everything seemed new and different to him.

"This land is really beautiful," he murmured. "It is," Isabella responded, as softly as he. "I am surprised you gave it up to stay in that house."

Luke shook his head. "He reached this stage before me. It was the right thing to do. I'll get land of my own." He looked down at her, feeling a surge of love for her pass through him. "For us. I'll get land for us. We'll both pick it out. And Lo can design the house we build on that land. We'll raise our kids there and then our grandkids and we'll die there. Together."

Isabella giggled, a sound he absolutely loved. "It sounds like you have our whole lives planned out."

"Not really," he responded softly. "The only thing

I know for certain is that we will spend it together. You and me. As partners. Just like you said."

Her smile radiated from her lips, drawing attention to them. Luke didn't have to hesitate anymore. He didn't have to wait for the right time. She was his wife. He could kiss her anytime he wanted.

With this thought in mind, he leaned in, pressing his lips against hers, letting his passion flow through him. He had her at first by the upper arms. As their loving kiss continued, he wrapped his arms around her. She lifted her hands to cup his shoulders, pushing herself against him so hard he could feel her heartbeat.

When they finally parted, they were both breathless. Luke didn't want to stop kissing her. He didn't care whether he could breathe or not. His love overwhelmed him, and he held her close.

"I love you, Izzie. My darling wife. My Isabella Turner." He chuckled, pulling back to look into her eyes. "That does sound strange, doesn't it?"

He could see the passion on her face. She shook her head and captured his heart all over again when she said, "It doesn't sound strange, my love. It sounds perfect. Utterly perfect."

EPILOGUE

All around her was laughing and dancing and music. Children ran around chasing each other. Bursts of laughter from random spots, both men and women, having a good time.

Isabella's eyes fell on her mother and father, who were dancing to the music on the dancefloor with several other couples. It was a lively tune, but not once that required much more than bouncing on one's feet. She left her eyes on the couple, thinking how even now, after all these years, they still smiled at each other like they'd been the ones to get married that day.

That's what Isabella wanted. And that, she was sure, was what she'd gotten.

Luke was somewhere around. After their private walk to the river, he'd decided to mingle but only after getting himself and Isabella a plate of food each. He said he couldn't have his wife fainting from starvation. That wouldn't make him a very good husband, would it?

She smiled as the memory passed through her mind. Someday she and Luke would be the ones dancing like her parents were. It was a shame Luke's weren't there to join in the celebration.

Isabella's smile grew wider when Luke popped up from behind a group of men. He didn't really pop "up". He popped "to the side". He had leaned over so far, she was surprised he hadn't fallen over. But he was now beaming at her with a playful grin. He mouthed and pointed at her. "You all right?"

She laughed under her breath and nodded. He nodded back and straightened himself, disappearing behind the tall men in between them.

"He's such a silly man sometimes." She heard Mattie next to her and turned her smile to her friend.

"Yes, he is. I am sure we will have a delightful time together."

"Oh, you will. I've seen his sense of humor since I've been with Dylan. And let me tell you, he's got a lot going on up here, too." Mattie dropped into the chair next to her, gesturing flamboyantly as she tapped her temple with one finger. "He's smart. And he has real good advice. It's because of him that Dylan changed his mind about all that stuff he believed."

Isabella blinked at Mattie, realizing her friend had indulged in a few glasses of champagne. She had no idea what Mattie was talking about but was highly curious to find out.

"I beg your pardon. What stuff was are you talking about?" The word "stuff" felt strange coming out of her mouth. She repeated it in her mind. It sounded funny to her. She made a mental note to use it more often.

"Oh, he used to believe all this nonsense about women being seen and not heard and the like," Mattie replied dismissively. "He doesn't think like that now."

"Luke shared those views?" This was surprising news to Isabella. She couldn't see her husband, but if she had been able to, she would have given him a curious look. Instead, she gave that look to Mattie.

Mattie shook her head, reaching around Isabella and picking up a glass of champagne that was half full. "No, he was the one who got

Dylan out of that way of thinking. I don't think he ever really thought that way. It's those fathers of theirs." Mattie drank the last of the champagne from the glass and put it down heavily. "I think I've had too much of that. I better go lie down."

Isabella wanted to hear more about the past she knew nothing about. But she could see her friend had clearly had too much to drink.

"I will help you. Come on."

She stood up, taking Mattie's hand and helping her walk straight.

Ten minutes later, she was coming back out of the house, having left Mattie in her large bed to sleep off her champagne consumption.

Luke was heading up toward the house from the shelter and saw her. An immediate look of delight came to his face, and he waved at her.

"There you are, my darling," he yelled out so loud she was sure people in the neighboring county had heard him.

Giggling, she went down the steps and crossed the lawn to meet him in the middle.

"I've been looking everywhere for you, dear. Where did you go?" he asked, resting his hands on her shoulders.

"I had to help Mattie. She had a little too much to drink and wanted to lie down."

Luke nodded. "Poor girl. She doesn't often drink now that she has a baby growing in her belly. She only had one. It must have hit her hard."

Isabella thought Mattie looked like she'd had more than one and visibly watched the young woman drink half a glass right in front of her. But it was true that she didn't drink often, and that probably was the reason for her current situation.

"She told me you and Dylan used to consider women to be seen and not heard." She wasn't sure she phrased that correctly but wanted to ask him about it, so she raised her eyebrows as if her non-question required an answer.

He blinked at her and leaned in close to place a quick kiss on her lips.

"Are you mad at me? If you're mad at me, it's awfully cute."

She giggled, shaking her head slightly, pressing herself against him. "I'm not mad. I'm just wondering why you would think that way."

Luke shrugged. "It wasn't really me. It was mostly Dylan. And when he fell in love, that all changed. It was mostly his pa and my pa that made us think like that. We were young men then."

Isabella grinned. "Two years ago? I believe that would be when you were young men?"

Luke laughed, and she joined him.

"Well, I will confess since you have confessed," Isabella continued.

Luke's grin vanished, and he gazed at her curiously.

"I am Dolly," she said bluntly.

He blinked some more, looking confused. "Who?"

Isabella laughed, throwing her head back. She lifted up on her toes and kissed him firmly on the mouth. "Dolly. Bean. The woman you wrote to in New York. I paid Andrew and Harry to keep mum while I left you a letter and took yours. You do forgive me, don't you?"

She watched his face as he realized what she was talking about and remembered what had happened.

He slapped a hand to his forehead. "I'd forgotten all about her. I mean, you. Oh, Izzie. You are the sweetest manipulator I've ever met."

Isabella laughed, but she tapped him on the nose and tried to give him a serious look. "I will never manipulate you again, Luke. I promise you this."

"And I believe you," he responded. "I love you, Izzie. With all my heart."

She hugged him, grateful for the warmth of his body when he returned it. "I love you, too, Luke. I always will."

Click here for more Blythe Carver books!

Sign up for the newsletter to be notified of new releases.

Click on link for
Newsletter
or put this in your browser window:

landing.mailerlite.com/webforms/landing/p6l2s1